W9-BDS-006

THE COFFINS
OF LITTLE HOPE

**Center Point
Large Print**

**This Large Print Book carries the
Seal of Approval of N.A.V.H.**

THE COFFINS
OF LITTLE HOPE

Timothy Schaffert

CENTER POINT LARGE PRINT
THORNDIKE, MAINE

This Center Point Large Print edition
is published in the year 2012 by arrangement with
Unbridled Books.

The text of this Large Print edition is unabridged.
In other aspects, this book may vary
from the original edition.
Printed in the United States of America
on permanent paper.
Set in 16-point Times New Roman type.

ISBN: 978-1-61173-304-4

Library of Congress Cataloging-in-Publication Data

Schaffert, Timothy.
 The coffins of Little Hope / Timothy Schaffert.
 p. cm.
 ISBN 978-1-61173-304-4 (library binding : alk. paper)
 1. Obituaries—Authorship—Fiction.
  2. City and town life—Nebraska—Fiction. 3. Missing persons—Fiction.
  4. Mothers and daughters—Fiction. 5. Nebraska—Fiction.
  6. Large type books. I. Title.
 PS3619.C325C64 2012
 813'.6—dc23
                                              2011038007

To R.R.

Part

· 1 ·

I still use a manual typewriter (a 1953 Underwood portable, in a robin's-egg blue) because the soft *pip-pip-pip* of the typing of keys on a computer keyboard doesn't quite fit with my sense of what writing sounds like. I need the hard metal clack, and I need those keys to sometimes catch so I can reach in and untangle them, turning my fingertips inky. Without slapping the return or turning the cylinder to release the paper with a sharp *whip,* without all that minor havoc, I feel I've paid no respect to the dead. What good is an obituary if it can be written so peaceably, so undisturbingly, in the dark of night?

Though my name does not begin with an S, my byline has always been S Myles because I'm Esther, but more often Essie, or Ess, and thus S (just S, no period) on the page.

· 2 ·

Our town, statistically, was the oldest it had ever been, population-wise. At eighty-three, I was years and years past a reasonable retirement age, but I'd never been so busy. We were all of us quite old, we death merchants—the town's undertaker (seventy-eight), his organist (sixty-seven), the desairologist (desairology: dressing

9

and ironing the hair of the deceased, manicuring their nails, rouging their cheeks with a simulated blush of heat; seventy-three), the florist (her freezer overgrown with lilies; eighty-one). The cemetery's caretaker, who procured for the goth high schoolers who partied among the tombstones, was the enfant terrible among us (at an immature fifty-six).

I'd chronicled the town's dead since dropping out of the eighth grade to work for my father, the publisher of the County Paragraph, a newspaper eventually to be run by my grandson, Doc (called Doc for his professorial carriage, in three-piece suits and neckties, and for his use of overly brainy words in his editorials, words lifted from a brittle-edged, outdated thesaurus in his top desk drawer). My first obit had not been meant as an obit but rather as an essay about my mother, who'd died giving birth to me. Throughout my childhood, I'd studied the sewing room my father had left untouched, and I'd stitched together a portrait of her based on notes she'd scribbled in the margins of recipe cards ("orange peel works too"), and on the particular velvet dress—with a patchwork of mismatched buttons—that had been left unfinished on the dressmaker's dummy, and on the postcards she'd had the bad habit of starting but not finishing (*Dear Millie* [her sister], *Just a fast, quick, short, unimportant note so I can get this into the mail before the carrier comes*—then nothing else).

You would think a woman in her eighties wouldn't cry for her mommy, and I don't really, it's really for the little girl that I was that I cry after I've had three or four whiskeys of an evening. But the weeping is pleasure. When I cry like a baby, my aches go, and I feel skinned, refreshed afterward. At that moment I'm happy to be sad and wish I could be so melancholy for hours. But it's fleeting. Sobriety is quick, and the night too long, and as I lie awake with sleeplessness, nervous from drink, I wish I hadn't drunk a drop.

· 3 ·

A nd this very book began not as a book but as an obit of a kind for a little girl who up and went missing one simple summer day. On this girl we pinned all hopes of our dying town's salvation. The longer we went without seeing her even once, the more and more dependent upon her we grew. She became our leading industry, her sudden nothingness a valuable export, and we considered changing the name of our town to hers; we would live in the town of *Lenore*. Is it any wonder that we refused to give up hope despite all the signs that she'd never existed, that she'd never been anybody—never, not even before she supposedly vanished?

By the time Daisy, the mother of that vaporous Lenore, finally called me to her farmhouse, after all the weeks of bickering and debate that enlivened our town yet ruined its soul, after most of the events of this book had passed, no one anywhere was any longer waiting for word of Lenore's death. It was the last Thursday of January, and the week had moved from an unseasonable thaw into a bitter chill that pained your teeth as you leaned into the wind. I went, alone, as requested, intending to help Daisy, as if plotting to steal her away from her own delusions. For some of us, Lenore was nothing but a captivating hoax, while for others, she was a grim tragedy, a mystery cynically left unsolved.

You were either one of the ones who truly believed in Lenore or you were one of the ones who believed in the same way you believe in the trickling stigmata of a plastic Virgin, with a trust in magic and miracle mostly for the thrill of it. Or you were one of the ones with no faith at all. Those were the ones, the ones with disbelief, who benefited the most, who made the most money on the sad pilgrims who skulked in and out of our town.

Some of you may say I'm just as bad as the worst of the people who've exploited the summer, fall, and winter of Lenore, that I've played this story like an accordion for the purposes of melodrama, squeezing and stretching, inflating and deflating scenes and events at will. You'll say I wasn't everywhere; you'll say there's no way I can know all that I've depicted. But I stand behind all the truths in this story of deception. Maybe because I've so long looked so old, even when I was relatively young, that people feel they can be revealing around me, that they can unbutton their lips and let slip intimate facts and trust that I have the maturity to keep my mouth shut.

· 4 ·

*W*hat *will you most remember?* It's a question I've asked of the grieving hundreds and hundreds of times. The people I ask almost always take a deep breath and exhale. "What will I most remember?" they most always say, looking up and off as they're thinking back. Their first responses, which come too quickly, simply to fill the silence in the room, are unexceptional: her infectious smile, his playful wink, her bubbly laugh, his gruff demeanor, which disguised his sweet, soft heart. But here's what I do: I write nothing down. I give them absolutely nothing, as if they've not yet said a word. I sit, my skinny legs crossed beneath my long skirt, my steno pad atop my knee, the point of my pen pressed on the paper but not moving, not even to doodle. They know that I know they can do better than that. To please me, then, they see past their grief and breathe vivid life back into their beloveds, in idiosyncratic detail.

What will they most remember about me? Will it be the cherry cough drops I constantly popped and the tart, antiseptic scent they gave my breath and the noise they made knocking against my teeth (my *death rattle,* my great-granddaughter lovingly calls it)? Because, you see, I've always been nervous among all the despair. And the older I've grown, the more nervous I've become.

Once upon a time, I could ease into a house of mourning as inconspicuously as a neighbor dropping off a coffee cake. An obit writer should not, by nature, be a memorable visitor. But when my crooked shadow falls across the doorstep, people likely think I've come grim-reaping. My hair is snow-white, and I'm quite tall, my head only just clearing some of the shorter of the doorjambs, even with an old-lady slouch I've had since girlhood. As a gangly teen, I thought it made me lady-like to curl in on myself. I thought it demure to lean forward into invisibility. All the admonishment I took from my concerned aunties for letting my hair fall in my face (*flirty-like,* one aunt said with disdain) failed to get me to straighten up, but I did take to wrenching it all back into a tight ponytail with silk ribbons, and I do still twist my knotted braids atop my head and riddle them with combs and clips and, my favorite, an ostentatious dragonfly hairpin bejeweled with colored glass. It's how people know me, for better or worse.

· 5 ·

The January afternoon I was summoned to Daisy's farm, on the pretense of writing Lenore's obit, Daisy welcomed me in and brushed the snow off my disgraceful fur coat, a mink that had long been on its last legs. She helped me to unravel the wool scarf I'd wrapped around my head, fussing with it when it caught on the wings of my dragonfly hairpin. She stuffed the scarf into a sleeve of my coat and hung the coat on the corner of the open closet door.

We sat at the kitchen table with cups of coffee, and after she told me stories of Lenore's childhood, all stories I'd heard before, she poured more coffee into my cup, though I'd yet to drink a sip. The coffee smelt burnt somehow, and it spilled over the brim. I held my hand above the rising steam in hopes of nursing my stiff joints.

Daisy pulled a thin cardigan tight over her shoulders. She wore a wispy blue dress meant for summer. She had a craggy, haggard beauty, all her troubles having taken their toll. Even sitting still and shivering, she had a bitter edge, a low-level fierceness. Middle age had rendered Daisy wasted and lovely both.

Daisy bit at the dry skin of her lip.

"Your lip's bleeding, sweetie," I said.

Daisy took the tissue tucked into the cuff of her sweater and dabbed at her lip. She pulled the tissue away to check the spot of blood, then dabbed again, then checked again. She kept dabbing and checking until the spots of blood shrank away.

"I know you're not going to print what I've told you," Daisy said, gesturing toward my notes in my steno pad, making a little scribbling motion in the air.

I removed my reading spectacles, partly for effect—like a doctor pained by the diagnosis he's delivering—and partly because of the glasses' weight on the bridge of my nose. I set them atop my notebook. "No," I said, "we won't print it." I took off my watch, heavy on my wrist. How many more winters until my bones simply shattered beneath the weight of my skin? I lifted the dragonfly hairpin from the knotted braid atop my head. The insect's hooked legs had felt snagged in my hair, yanking at my scalp with my every nod. "I won't be writing an obituary for Lenore."

"Then what'd you come here for?" Daisy said, looking up at me with genuine interest.

"I thought it might help you," I said. "I want to

help you." *Help her,* I thought, sneering to myself, even then. We were the ones who'd done all the damage, every last one of us. How could any of us help? I unclasped the cluster of rhinestones clipped to my left earlobe, a cumbersome piece of costume jewelry, and placed it among my other things. I hear best with that ear. "Daisy, I think you're hurt, is what I think. I think your heart is broken. Do you think my heart's never been broken? I know what such a thing does. If there's *anything* I know from this life, I know what heartbreak does."

Daisy said nothing, only stared at my undrunk cup of coffee. I then felt compelled to drink it. I leaned over to sip off the excess before lifting the cup. The coffee tasted humid, like the smell of a dishcloth left in the sink.

"Okay, I'll tell you the truth, Mrs. Myles," Daisy said.

"Please," I said, putting my chin in my hand and leaning forward, my good ear out.

"I lied," she said. "I don't really think Lenore is dead. I wanted you to write her obituary, and to print it, to wake everybody up. People would be disgusted by it, an obit for Lenore; I know they would. And they'd care about her again. Because, Mrs. Myles, I know he didn't kill her. He loved her. That's why he took her. She's somewhere alive, and afraid."

Finally a tear rolled down her cheek and over

the pout of her lower lip. I was unmoved. Maybe I didn't want to help her at all. Maybe I just wanted to hear a confession, and I wanted to be the one to tell the truth to others. If I live to be a hundred, I'll still have this infantile need to know everything before everyone else.

None of this was an effort toward closure. It seemed just another beginning in a story that was all beginnings. And that was probably why my little town couldn't get enough of it. We were so tired of endings.

Part

B ut if we were to begin at the beginning, we would need to begin, strangely enough, with a book, the eleventh book in an eleven-book series. Many of you have read it at least once by now, whether aloud to a child at bedtime or simply to yourself. The eleven-book saga took years to unfold, invoking nightmares among generations of children. Many otherwise stable men and women well into their forties still feel struck with the heebie-jeebies when they recall the gothic predicaments of the two sisters, Miranda and Desiree, the innocent wards of Rothgutt's Asylum for Misguided Girls.

The eleventh book was long anticipated. We were finally to learn the fate of Miranda and Desiree, who'd spent the first ten books longing for their mother to come and collect them from the dank, infested halls of Rothgutt's. Even if you had never read a word of the Miranda-and-Desirees, it was impossible not to be versed in the language of the books, and their characters and places, and to be curious about how it all might end.

The first Miranda-and-Desiree books were morbid curiosities with small print runs, but eventually mad housewives in Middle America challenged the books at their local libraries. The books worked their way up the national banned books lists; they went up in smoke in bonfires fueled by zealots. When one First Lady took as her cause a campaign against violence in children's entertainment and censured the Miranda-and-Desirees for their inappropriate carnival of calamities, it was as if the publisher had rigged the lottery.

And that was how my family's newspaper, the County Paragraph, came to use its press to print a portion of the Miranda-and-Desiree novels. The series' publisher was a company in New York called Henceforth Books, and it was seeking presses in obscure parts of the country where it could covertly print the novels, avoiding the security breaches that had led to thieved copies, details leaked, plots spoiled. Executives of Henceforth consulted a Washington Post article called "The Last Gasps of the Small-Town Chronicle," in which the Paragraph was profiled among several little-town Tribunes, Republics, Heralds, Independents, Sentinels, and Optimists.

Doc, my grandson, was unhappy with the article—he'd been painted with a broad brush as a tad hapless, having built, in the country, a massive new state-of-the-art press, anticipating contracts with other area publications—a miscalculation, as newspapers decades old, some of them more than a century old, toppled all around us with minimal fanfare.

Though Doc foolishly underbid in his

determination to become one of the several small-town publishers printing the books, and foolishly expanded the press's equipment to allow for the particulars of book publishing—the binding and the sewing and the finishing of the spine—the deal did manage to keep the press from getting mauled by its own gears. And had not the books become central to our conversations about Lenore, we would likely still be keeping mum about our involvement, just as we had since we'd first contracted with Henceforth Books, our confidentiality clauses quite rigid. When the books were being printed, the factory lights were dimmed to prevent workers from seeing so much as a single word; employees were subjected to pat-downs and searches of their lunch boxes by private security firms sent in by Henceforth. Midnight trains chugged up along rarely used tracks at the back of the factory, our forklifts cradling the boxes of books into the cars, to be delivered to the world. All that activity, and all that employment, and none of us breathed a word of it to anyone.

· 7 ·

Before Lenore vanished, Daisy worked at our printing factory, though none of us really knew her. She biked to the press in the early mornings and biked away in the early afternoons.

She ate her lunch on a bench in the yard in the summer, and in the winter she ate on the floor in the hallway. She wasn't beloved for her eccentricity, but she wasn't hated for it either.

A man who Daisy called Elvis, because of his Vegas-style pompadour and sexy drawl, came to the door of her farmhouse the summer that the pages of the final Miranda-and-Desiree rolled secretly through the tumblers and cylinders of our press.

He stood at her door on a night in June with his denim shirt all unsnapped down the front, offering to help her clear the farm of the branches that a tornado had ripped from the trees and tossed asunder. He stayed in Daisy's house, and he was so good with Lenore, she claimed, so good that it broke her heart to think how long Lenore had been without a father figure. He waited for Daisy every evening in the parking lot of the printing press, and they would ride back to her farm, the two of them on her bike, wobbling along. He would ask her to describe the work she did, and she'd tell him how important it was, with this particular book, to manage the flow of the ink to the inking rollers. "It's a special ink, I guess," she said; "not a drop should be wasted"—an ink concocted of blueberries and carrots and kelp.

"You'll be guilty of theft," Elvis said one midnight, flipping over the next card in a stack of tarot. He and Daisy sat on her bed, a week or so before he left with Lenore, and Elvis told her fortune. The moon cast enough light against the bed to see by. Playful, he predicted for her a shellfish allergy, braces on her teeth, and a tawdry affair with a bearded lady.

It was sweltering in the house—a sultry, humid July night—and Elvis had stripped down to his boxers, and Daisy had put on a ratty, threadbare baby doll. They sucked on chips of ice.

"Theft," Daisy said, surprising Elvis with a page of the final book, taking it from where she'd stashed it between the mattress and the box spring. The book would not be in bookstores, would not be read, until winter, months away. Back at the factory, the page had gotten caught and torn and mangled in the feed. All the ink smeared. They could barely read any of the words, and the words they could read didn't make any sense because they all just bled into a molasses of black. At the factory, Daisy had stuck the folded paper into the front of her jeans, against the skin of her stomach, where she wouldn't get pawed and patted by security. Daisy and Elvis studied the paper marked with letters stretched and colliding, words running on top of each other, tangling, losing shape and meaning.

· 8 ·

A LITTLE FAMILY TREE:

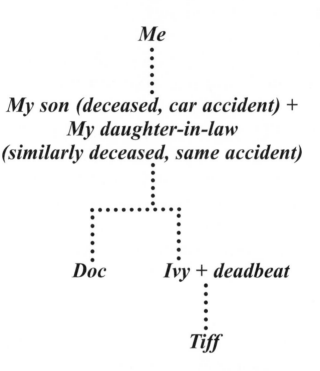

Me

My son (deceased, car accident) +
My daughter-in-law
(similarly deceased, same accident)

Doc   *Ivy + deadbeat*

Tiff

My grandson, Doc, lived with his niece, Tiff (short for Tiffany), in a little house across the street from me, a house they'd named the Artichoke Heart, for its green shingles. Doc's sister, Tiff's mother, had abandoned Tiff and fled to Paris six years before. It hadn't surprised any of us when Ivy had just up and left; what had surprised us was that she'd been so devoted to Tiff for the first seven years of the girl's life. Ivy had not been a junkie or a drunk—she'd been too uncommitted to anything to be an addict of any kind.

There's a pioneer graveyard out in the country, one you have to know about to find, as it's tucked far back off the road and hidden by the drape of overgrown weeping willows. On the afternoon of Lenore's disappearance, before we knew of all that was to possess us, Tiff and I went to the graveyard. I let Tiff drive once we turned off the paved roads. She had to stretch her leg and tippy her toes to press at the gas. She drove slowly, unbearably slowly, but when I snapped at her to speed up, she snapped back. "Please, Essie!" she said. "You make me too damn nervous!" But it was endless, her driving.

Tiff and I stopped at the railroad tracks to pick wildflowers from the ditch to take to the cemetery to decorate the graves. A century of rain had worn away many of the names on the limestone, but dates remained, and Tiff held paper against the stone and ran a piece of charcoal over it to make rubbings of the most tragic dates—six days; eight days; two months. She made rubbings of carvings of babies with wings and of children riding on the backs of lithe dogs. She took pictures with a semi-expensive digital camera Doc had given her to encourage ambitions in journalism.

As she snapped photos of an angel with no dots in her marble eyes, I sat on a stone bench, my back against a wrought-iron gate. A plump bumblebee bounced off my sleeve. "Bee!" I said, waving it away, and Tiff turned her camera on me. Tiff then showed me, in the little window in the back of her camera, the sight of me flustered, my eyes buggy, the bee nowhere.

"What if the bee had stung me," I said, "and it had turned out I'm fatally allergic? Having made it through my entire life, allergic to stings but never stung—would that seem like luck, even as I died?"

"I don't know," Tiff said, "but I basically would've captured your murder on camera." She raised one eyebrow and rocked on the balls of her feet. "Would I have clicked *delete,* or would I have kept it and looked at it over and over and over for the rest of my life?"

"And would you have told anyone that you'd taken such a picture," I said, "or would you have felt somehow responsible?"

"You know, the thing is, I think I would've kept the picture," she said, squinting, thinking. "But I don't think I would've ever been able to look at it. It would've just always been there, and I'd always just kind of see it in my head. I would always *want* to look at it, like, I'd always be tempted to freak myself out with it, but I never would except, you know, once or twice maybe."

"And you would've always felt guilty thinking how if you'd just shooed the bee away instead of stopping to immortalize my fatal battle with it . . ."

"Ack," she said, "now I'm getting the creeps. *Deleeeete.*" And she erased the picture cleanly with a press of her thumb. I then posed for a proper photo after punching up the purplish-red of my lips with a few fresh dots of lipstick.

She turned her camera around for me to see my picture, and I couldn't quite take my eyes off myself, but not out of vanity, I don't think. And I don't think it was just because I'm so enamored of my great-granddaughter. You go through life exposed to so many snapshots of yourself looking half undone that when you see one that's flattering—your hair just as you'd combed it, your blouse fitting how you'd hoped for it to fit—it's like you've witnessed something long unknown about yourself. I was tempted to think I'd been pretty all along.

Back at home, we investigated each other for ticks, the tall grass of the cemetery always so thick with them. As we sat on the sofa in our silk kimonos, we found two of the parasites with their fangs already sunk in.

That summer of Lenore, Tiff was burned dark from the sun, and the tiny hairs on her leg were so blond they were nearly clear. Tiff could lose herself in my skin too, preoccupied by my arms and hands, by the wrinkles and spots and a stray hag-like hair curling up from a knuckle. She pushed, with her fingertips, at the flesh of my wrist, the skin slippery on the bone.

· 9 ·

Doc and his sister, Ivy, had been very close growing up. The two had not been tragically orphaned—they'd both been in their twenties when their parents' car had slid off a tall, wet bridge. But Doc inherited the County Paragraph much too young, and it all possessed an urgency that distracted him. He took to wearing a linen suit and straw porkpie hat, elements of style that, in my honest opinion, hurt him in the community. Such dandification was why our readers preferred not to take him seriously. They'd loved his father's editorials, his gentle turns of phrase and patriarchal commonsense. His father had been practiced in his plainspokenness. And though the neckties Doc wore to work were from his father's collection of garish, hand-painted ties bought on vacations (leggy Vegas showgirls in midkick, hula dancers with hibiscus bras) that had endeared Doc's father to everyone and rendered him approachable and unpretentious—on Doc they looked affected.

Ivy, meanwhile, fell into despair, feeling bereft not just of her parents but of Doc, now so newly responsible. Doc was fascinated by his sister, and he'd always been a willing audience for her every mad turn and dizzy spell. I'd long felt that Ivy's incapacity for everyday life was put on for Doc's benefit. She was mesmerized by his sympathy.

Ivy mourned her parents by falling in love, dangerously so, with a man beautiful but demented, and she then became pregnant. Tiff doesn't now even have a photo of her father because Ivy burned any pictures to an ash that she then spread ceremoniously across the dirt of the teacup roses she'd planted in memory of her mother.

In Ivy's sudden absence, seven-year-old Tiff showed all the classic signs of abandonment—bed-wetting, sleepwalking, heartbreaking crying jags. But Doc, in my very biased opinion, quickly took her mother's place. Ivy never called, never remembered a birthday. Once a postcard from Avignon arrived with a melodramatically illegible scrawl—"Tiff, Please never forget me," she'd written, so clearly engrossed in her own fiction of herself. I wanted to write back to her to tell her we'd all laughed. We hadn't laughed, though. We'd wandered around in a funk for days, saddened that we'd had to be reminded of her and her indifference.

Doc and Tiff established their own traditions, and even now they still sit in the yard on Sundays, in sunglasses, on a blanket, reading aloud to each other, intensely, from books of instruction for magicians. Through catalogs, online sites, and road trips to estate auctions, they amassed closets full of tricks and a basement of magic cabinets.

They had capes with hidden pockets and a magician's assistant's skimpy, feathery getup, its pink plumage mangy, having been nibbled away to sticks by dust mites. They stalked the yard's doves and rabbits in order to test their false-bottomed birdcages and collapsible top hats. They played poker with decks with five aces, lit firecrackers to produce silk carnations with an innocuous *pop*. They plucked coins from each other's nostrils, rubber mice from their ears, and miles of knotted-up scarves from their comically gaping mouths.

It had been Doc's dream, since his childhood, to open a magic shop. As a boy, he'd had no interest in working for the newspaper; rather, he'd pictured himself in a city of theaters. Whenever an illusionist needed a new fake thumb for his finger hatchet or a mirrored box for the segmenting of his assistant, Doc would be the supplier in this dream city of his. He'd have insights into all the sturdiest accoutrements of professional trickery, but he'd also serve the novice, the hobbyist, by offering the most convincing spyglasses, the foulest pepper gum.

In Tiff he'd found a worthy acolyte. She was fellow magician, assistant, and randomly selected audience member, all in one. By the time her mother returned from France, Tiff had mastered skills of invisibility. Tiff could still herself with an eerie precision, softening her heartbeats and stopping her breath. She'd go fetal in order to curl herself into the narrowest nook or cranny.

It was the summer Lenore went missing that our Ivy returned. With inheritance and insurance money that she'd miraculously avoided squandering, Ivy bought a house a few blocks from our houses. She painted it pink, as Tiff had requested, though Tiff had been mostly joking when she'd suggested it. At the café, where we would go for roast-beef sandwiches and cups of strong coffee, Ivy would order in French, then giggle before correcting herself.

"You can move back in with me whenever you're ready," she told Tiff the day she arrived with gifts of new dresses, much too small, which Tiff dutifully modeled, leaving the buttons undone up the back or shrugging her shoulders to give her arms the appearance of not being too long for the sleeves.

Ivy fashioned a bedroom for Tiff, gluing glow-in-the-dark stars to the ceiling and painting clouds on the walls, all in her approximation of what she thought a girl like Tiff might like. "I'll let you know the second it's ready," she told Tiff, and we waited, curious about ourselves, wondering what we'd all do once the room was finished.

· 10 ·

Tiff stopped eating then, and none of us noticed. We spent the summer, as usual, devoted to gluttony, grilling steaks and pillaging our vegetable gardens—frying green beans in bacon and grease, roasting sweet corn. I sliced cucumbers and onions and let them soak in sugar and vinegar, and Ivy used fresh beet juice to bloody the red velvet cakes she baked.

Then, into this summer idyll, the lifeguard of the swimming pool, a spunky, slight teenaged girl probably no stranger to anorexia herself, stopped by Doc's to ask him if he'd noticed how sharp Tiff's shoulder blades were looking lately, and how knobby her knees.

"I eat!" Tiff shouted, protesting beyond all reason when we confronted her at dinner. "I eat like a pig!" She *oink*ed noisily, puffing out her cheeks, a childishness that was unlike her. As we looked at her then, we saw what we hadn't been seeing—our girl turning skeletal. We'd been so distracted by our own obsessing over what was best for Tiff that we'd let her drop from our sights. Whenever Ivy had been at the table with us, which had been often that summer, we'd been embarrassed by her clumsy, coquettish pursuit of her daughter's affections, and we'd looked everywhere but at each other, tracing our fingers

34

over the monograms stitched into our napkins or watching the funhouse stretch of our reflections in the bowls of our spoons.

The night we accused her of starving herself, I asked her if she'd walk me to my door across the street. I linked my arm with hers, but she snatched hers back when she sensed me weighing the extent of her scrawniness, my fingertips considering the bone of her elbow.

"My sister, Lydia, quit eating one summer," I recalled. "She insisted only on watermelon so she could pee it all away." I hadn't thought about it in years. Lydia had been a teenager, and though there'd been only five years' difference between us, she'd seemed, in her distance and mystery, far more sophisticated than I'd sensed I'd ever be. The starvation had lent Lydia even more gravity and refinement, despite how peaked and sunken-cheeked she'd grown by August. "The only reason my father worried was because he thought no one would marry her because 'Who wants to marry a girl who looks like an old lady already?' Back then, nobody thought a girl like that might need some help. We just thought she was being stubborn. Nobody knew what anorexia was, or anything like that."

Tiff stopped in the middle of the street, closed her eyes tight, and grabbed her head. "Oh. My. Gawwwwww-duh," she wailed. "I am *not* anorexic."

"No, no, no, I know, I know you're not, sweetie," I said, but I swiftly ended with my denial, uncertain whether I might be making matters worse. You can always make matters worse these days, no matter where your heart is. When I was a young parent, we never used the word *parenting*. The only bad parents were parents with bad children. Now a parent can be doing the wrong thing even when she's doing the right thing. We've all come to know too well the psychology of childhood.

"I just get a stomachache sometimes," she said. She sighed. "A firefly," she said then, reaching up with her fingertip as if she might be able to tap its light back on.

"They're as thick as mosquitoes this summer," I said, and certainly, there they all were as we looked up and down the street, the insects' slow, delicate sparks giving the evening its character. "I'm a terrible cook," I said. "It's as simple as that. That's why you can't eat. You're being poisoned. Who could blame you?" Tiff rolled her eyes, and she took my arm and led me from the street and up my front walk. "Lydia could cook," I said. "She even cooked for my daddy and me during her hunger strike. That summer that she was starving herself, she stuffed us to the gills. To distract us, maybe. I think we were half asleep half the time, we ate so much and so often. Oh, how Lydia could cook before she got old. If she could still cook, you'd eat. You'd gorge yourself."

"You wouldn't worry I was too thin; you'd worry I was too fat," she said.

"I'd worry you were too fat, yes, probably," I said, and as I touched again at her arm and felt her lean against me, I wondered if it were too wistful and naive to hope that Tiff might make it through life neither too fat nor too thin and perhaps entirely undamaged in general.

Part

THREE

The farm on which the girl Lenore was said to have lived was a patchwork of agricultural projects: minor orchards and mostly fruitless gardens. A forest of evergreens, intended for Christmas, trudged up one side of a low hill and down the other, each tree long since too big for any house. Daisy's father had planted them, and he'd died before they'd grown. The trees' branches stretched up and out, the air around them thick with the medicinal gin-scent of juniper. Back when the evergreens had been right-sized for a holiday, no families in parkas had come with their little axes, so the trees, unsold, continued to grow and grow, overgrowing any potential, darkening the paths of dry needles beneath them.

And along a trellis, a vineyard had perished, the plants choked one summer by the herbicides carried over on the wind from a neighboring farm. Now all that remained were the knobby sticks of dried vines.

A narrow plank that hung from a few thin chains at the farm's entrance bore the name of the farm—the Crippled Eighty—which had been burned into the wood, in that shivery, lasso-like, cowboy cursive, with a wood-burning kit by Daisy's father. But the farm had actually been named, in mockery, by Daisy's mother, long before Lenore was even born (if, indeed, she'd been born at all). "Nothing will grow," the woman had told her husband. "It's eighty acres of hills," she'd said. She hadn't even looked at the landscape as she'd stood in the sun, squinting instead at her reflection in a small mirror, the glass of it dusted with aspirin that had broken at the bottom of her pocketbook. She'd dabbed on lipstick as she'd spoken. "You bought the only acreage within miles that doesn't have an inch of flatness. What are you going to do? Grow olive trees?"

But the land, uncrippled after all, had come to life for Daisy's father, and for thirty years there'd been a lush harvest of corn one summer, beans the next, then corn again; there'd been cattle, hogs, chickens, eggs, milk. There'd been pasture choked with musk thistle and a narrow creek that had always made Daisy think of the baby Moses shoved off in a thatched basket. At least that was how things had been before Daisy's mother had left the farm.

Daisy, a woman none of us had known at all well, told all this to Doc. She trusted Doc to tell her story. From the very beginning, she confided in him, and as Doc featured her on his front page week after week, and as the newspaper gained new subscribers not just from the region but from far beyond, far even outside the United States, his was the voice most closely associated with the facts and fictions of Lenore's disappearance.

While other writers from other towns approached the subject with big-city insensitivity, their every word a coy wink, Doc lent Lenore a beating heart.

Lenore's absence only days old, Daisy took Doc on a tour of the farm. Here, she told him, was a stump where Lenore sat and startled spiders and let them bite her so she could watch the effect of their venom; here was Lenore's own patch of garden, where she tried to grow things no one else in the local countryside grew, from seeds sent in the mail and fertilized with bat guano: tomatillos as hard and bitter as green apples; a Mexican melon with thorns on its skin. Tiny, foreign tomatoes, still plentiful on the vine that July afternoon, tasted like mango.

Nonetheless, the County Paragraph gave voice to its share of skeptics. *Spiders bit her!* a local wrote in a letter published on the Letters page. *Lenore wasn't kidnapped! She died! Daisy buried her in the pasture! Take a shovel and turn up that garden of exotic vegetables, and you'll find Lenore's corpse!*

· *12* ·

The people of our town learned, from the County Paragraph, details about the night before Daisy discovered Lenore gone: a rusted-out pickup, its tireless wheels up on blocks, downhill from the house among other scrap metal—junked tractors, bent fence posts, the shell of a Studebaker filled with leafy cocklebur plants. Elvis would become famous by the police artist's sketch, his eyes sleepy and heavy-lidded. In the sketch, he had a kind of beard, and we debated what to call it—was it a Vandyke or a goatee? Was it an overgrown soul patch? Across his forehead fell a forelock, a sweep of thick, dark curl that we knew was the thing that was probably most seductive. How do you see past such a cute lick of boyishness? We could imagine it coming loose always and flopping forward, distracting and handsome. And he was handsome, in a way, truth be told, even with that creepy pout the artist gave him. There were more than just a few among us who thought they could easily have seen past that silly beard long enough to fall in love. Some of us had fallen for worse, of course.

"You probably think I'm a child," Daisy had told Elvis, down the hill from the house. The truck had been lit by the moon. She'd sat on the passenger side, barefoot, in a lime-green dress of a gauzy material patterned with daisies. Elvis had bought the dress for her from a boutique in the city.

Her mother had given parties with daisies frosted on cakes, daisies on the paper napkins and Dixie cups, real daisies in vases—the wrapping paper of presents had had daisies, smiling cartoon daisies with fluttery loves-me-loves-me-not eyelashes, and inside had been plush daisies on the toes of bedroom slippers, daisies in the corners of stationery, on a springtime raincoat and rain boots.

But Daisy thanked Elvis, with kisses and kisses, for the dress he brought her, because how could he know? After all, she had nothing with daisies now; they didn't even grow in her flower patch.

Daisy sat with her knees together, her hair bobby-pinned in a futile effort to control its frazzle. She held the cold bottle on top of her knee. "You think I'm a nervous little girl for not wanting to drink in the house," she said. Elvis had bought the bottles of hard lemonade for the evening, and the drink, though weak, got Daisy tipsy fast. She never drank except when Elvis was on the farm. And he'd only been there a few times before, for a few days at a time, over the last few years. So whenever she drank with him, it went right to her head.

"You *are* a little girl," Elvis said. He held the bottle to her mouth, then kissed her wet lips. He put his hand to her head and pulled her close to his chest. He had muscles in his arms, and his T-shirt smelled of pipe tobacco. "That's why Daddy loves you, right? Daddy loves his little girl, doesn't he? Daddy loves Daisy."

In her comfort, resting against him, she told about sitting in this pickup years ago, waiting for her father by the irrigation pond, deep in the field. She'd been young enough to have no sense of the expanse of the world, and she'd imagined herself in a jungle, continents and continents away from home—immersed in the lush green, and the bugs that bit and itched the skin, and the chorus of toads that creaked their foreign noise.

As she continued to talk and talk and talk to Elvis, she told him about her father in the months before his death thirteen years before. She told about him sitting at the end of the vegetable garden, in a rusted metal folding chair, pointing his cane at potato plants for Daisy to dig up. As she'd shoveled and harvested throughout the garden, she'd found herself watching and listening very closely to her father; she'd sensed something fatal in his every flinch and cough.

"I'll never leave you," Elvis told her, and Daisy loved just leaning against him, leaning into him, the muffled thump of his heart in her ear pressed against his chest. She hadn't wanted to drink in the house and hadn't wanted Lenore to hear her with Elvis, to hear her whimper in his arms and to beg him to call her his baby. It'd been bad enough that Lenore had seen her sit in Elvis's lap as he'd read aloud from a fraudulent Miranda-and-Desiree novel he'd bought from a street vendor in Hong Kong, a piece of apocrypha that fell between books six and seven, in which Miranda and Desiree find and saddle an extinct Tasmanian tiger and rescue a family of orphans who'd been locked away in a grandfather clock. Elvis collected everything—all the counterfeit books bought in other countries, the miles of pages of fan fiction online, the encyclopedias of characters and associations and devices, the dolls, the movies, the board games, the cereal boxes, the comic books, the first two seasons of the animated series on DVD, and the DVDs' hour after hour of extras.

When Lenore had fallen asleep, Daisy and Elvis had walked to the old pickup behind the tin lean-to in the feedlot. She'd carried her shoes in her hand, though the grass was dry and burned-up, sharp against her bare feet.

After they'd stepped into the pickup, as Elvis pried open the bottle tops of the hard lemonade against the steering wheel, Daisy checked herself in the rearview mirror. So very plain, she thought.

To desire and to be desired was the best part of it all. Sex left Daisy feeling greedy—she could never get close enough. She'd rather stay in the quiet moments leading up to it. She wanted to be whispered to, all his little promises. She would, every night that he was there, lie with his arms around her, her back to his chest, cradled, and he'd fall asleep first, his hold growing sweetly slack, his breath going slow. She loved staying awake long enough to lose him like that.

It was already the middle of July, but a few leftover fireworks nonetheless popped and spun in the black sky, shot off by kids on adjacent farms. Daisy and Elvis drank and watched. This time, Daisy fell asleep first.

· *13* ·

In the morning Elvis was gone, and Lenore was gone too. Or, as many might say, she was not gone at all but suddenly there, newly sprung from her mother's imagination.

What woke Daisy in the early morning wasn't the racket of the airplane's motor but rather the tickle of the pickup seat she lay against. A mouse scurried beneath the vinyl, tiny among the rusty springs, working into Daisy's dream about sleeping on the kitchen floor. A chill shimmied up her spine from the thought of the mouse, and she sat up just soon enough to see the plane lift into the sky and only just clear the electrical lines at the tops of the poles.

Elvis was an aerial photographer, flying from town to town across the country's farmlands—he would take photos of a home place from far enough above to capture several verdant acres, to offer a rare view of rooftops, and rows of corn bins, and the geodesic patterns in the colors of the crops. But somehow, also, and this was his gift, he'd bring out some fine detail that made the

48

photo more than just a view of a farm from a few miles up. In a photo of the Ruskind place, you can see the dots of Mrs. Ruskind's prize Whirly-Girl tomatoes, still only a lemony orange in midsummer, like freckles, in the vegetable garden near the house. In the photo of the Jansenn farm, there's the family's snow-white husky, since dead from a sudden liver failure, a blur, chasing a passing car. Sunflowers along fence lines, pale green apples visible in the dark green leaves of trees. In these photos taken from a distance, Elvis allowed farmers a new intimacy with their own homes.

Elvis would develop the photos, put them in fancy gilt frames, and peddle them door to door, asking you to pay for pictures of your own place. He'd wear a charmingly outdated denim leisure suit, with a pair of aviator sunglasses pushed up on the top of his head. His hair was just a tad too long, tucked behind his ears. Women were happy to invite him in for a cup of coffee (but he preferred tea, Darjeeling if you happened to have it), and he might stay for an hour, or longer, complimenting your needlepoint or demanding your recipe for the rhubarb pudding cake you cut him a slice or two of. By the time you wrote the check, you hated to see him leave.

This was all before, though, a few years before, during his other sweep through town, before he cultivated the Vegas-style pompadour and whatever kind of beard that was. We didn't know his name—some of us remembered him as Kip; others remembered him as Jeb; others seemed to think his name was Mickey. Kim, Hank, Dusty, Max, Seymour. Some of us insisted his name was Cash, as that was who we all made our checks out to.

But the farm wives did remember, vividly, some other names—the women's names on his arms. Because Elvis calculated his sales calls so they'd fall when only the missus was likely to be home, he'd at some point take off his jacket, revealing short sleeves and the names tattooed and crossed out up his forearm. ~~Vicki~~. ~~Mitzi~~. ~~Veronica~~. ~~Lois~~. It might have been his idea of a joke, but the women liked entertaining the thought of him falling so passionately, so permanently for these temporary loves.

All the winking and drawling he did, the effortless romancing of the women in and around our town, probably didn't help Daisy's case, especially when she told her stories to the newspaper—all that "Daddy" and "Baby" business, all that *Baby needs her daddy*. It sounded perverse to the women in our town, but, worse yet, many of them were jealous. No, no, worse than that: they were regretful. Why, for God's sake, had they led the lives that had led them to sit there, dusting their thimble collections or stirring ice cubes into their Jell-O mixes, while

50

this pretty-lipped freak sat, sex on the brain, wrinkling the doilies on their sofas? Why did that very strange woman, only a few farms over, get to be the one to be violated? All any of the farm wives would have had to do was reach over and flick a few top buttons of his shirt to see his hairy chest—they'd all been within arm's reach of complete self-destruction. Why wasn't it themselves they were reading about in the morning papers?

Not that anyone could love a man who would endanger a child. And that was why it was easy for some of us to cast Lenore into nothingness. Elvis had not abducted a little girl. He loved *women*. We all knew that by the names on his arm—they were women's names. There were no little girls anywhere, anymore, named Mitzi or Veronica.

· 14 ·

Daisy, at first, felt no panic when Lenore was nowhere to be found. It wasn't unusual for Lenore to wake early, to walk to the peach trees to see if the fruit was still too green to eat. *That one,* Daisy would tell the sheriff later, pointing at a peach on a low-hanging branch, when they were trying to piece together a clinical portrait of Lenore's existence—seeking a single strand of hair, a bit of skin that had flaked from a peeling, sunburned shoulder. Anything. Any sliver of soap or chewed-up plug of gum stuck beneath the seat of a kitchen chair. *Didn't you ever snip off a curl to tape onto a page of her baby book?*

This peach, Daisy said, reaching out to cradle it in the palm of her hand, careful not to disturb its precious place in the investigation. It was all she had, she knew. *The skin's broken there, just slightly,* she explained. She put her thumb to where the peach was bruised, its skin nicked. *That's where Lenore pressed at it with her fingernail. She was seeing if it was soft enough to eat yet. See? That's Lenore. She was here.*

· *15* ·

Lenore," she called out the back door. "Lenore, come to the house. I know you can hear me." Still undisturbed, she returned to Lenore's room and picked up from the floor the book that had been propping open the window. *A Prairie Wedding Among the Radishes*, by Myrtle Kingsley Fitch. The local library was sponsoring a citywide read that summer, and we were all to read, and to discuss, *A Prairie Wedding*, a suitably musty bit of Pulitzer-winning frump from 1918. In the band shell at the park, Dr. Tanya Krelb, the Myrtle Kingsley Fitch Professor of English at the state university, gave a talk about the symbolism in the book—explaining what the pumpkin blossoms meant, and what it meant that a woman's father was murdered at a bend in the river, and how we were to interpret the creaking of the katydids, the sound of which she mimicked with the aid of a wooden whistle hand-carved from cedar, though many of us thought she sounded more like a locust. "Myrtle Kingsley Fitch is your sister," the suspiciously unbridal Dr. Tanya Krelb told us, "her land is your land," explaining that Myrtle Kingsley Fitch had grown up in our state, only miles from our town. Had Lenore not disappeared in July to distract us, we all would've been subjected to an autumn book festival.

Daisy opened the window, putting the book back on the sill to keep the window up. "Lenore," she called out, and it was then, her calls met only with the stillness of the Crippled Eighty, the quiet noise the land had likely been making for centuries, that she first felt the loss of her daughter. She felt it in her stomach, a quick rush. She listened closer, trying to convince herself that the sound of the wind brushing the pasture grass was Lenore walking slowly up from the creek, knee-deep in the weeds. Her heart leaped with relief with the noise of a bird that sounded like a toy, the wings clacking, slapping, like wings made of wood.

"Lenore," Daisy shouted, wanting Lenore to hear the shake in her voice so she'd know she'd gone too far with her hide-and-seek. Daisy cried as she circled the house twice, casting her sight everywhere, trying to look at every inch of every acre. "I'm so angry right now, Lenore," she shouted, but she wasn't. She was terrified. Elvis's attention to Lenore took on a different tenor in her memory. *I could just eat you up,* he'd say, pinching her cheek. *You deserve the best of everything,* he'd say.

· *16* ·

Within the thick of a cornfield, the musk of vegetation filled her mouth with breath almost too damp for her lungs to take in, and Daisy feared she'd never get to the outer edge. She felt covered in insects, even tasted them, and as she stomped through the dirt, cutting the skin of her bare feet, she slapped away the spotted, lime-colored rootworm beetles crawling on her arms and neck and legs. She picked them from her tongue and her teeth. The cornstalks, so tall and peaceful, rattling only gently with the slight wind and Daisy's movement, sliced at her, their smooth leaves leaving paper-cut slashes across her flesh.

When Daisy stepped from the cornfield, she could've gone left or she could've gone right. If she'd gone right, her story would've changed so radically that there might've been no story at all. It would've been so easy to dismiss her had she gone right, a little less than forty feet down the highway, to one of our town's oldest institutions:

"Peeping" Tom's Liquor and Discount Cigarettes. "Peeping" Tom's that fateful day was staffed solely by a twenty-two-year-old who spent his work hours eating Cherry Mash candy and leaving his chocolate fingerprints on the pages of the store's dirty magazines.

But Daisy didn't go right; she went left, to the Garden of Gethsemane Lutheran Church, even though it was much farther away, practically a quarter mile, and the black asphalt of the highway felt like a hot iron pressed against her bare, bleeding feet.

The church's Board of Elders, a claque of old men, happened to be meeting that morning, and they happened to be meeting in the chapel, not the fellowship hall as usual, rendering Daisy's entrance into their lives all the more dramatic. They'd gone into the chapel, in their finest suits and newest ties, to confront the young minister, who was at the lectern rehearsing his sermon, a particularly rabid piece of fire-and-brimstone in which he intended to blame us all for all the recent acts of God—tornadoes that had decimated area farms in May, more tornadoes that had killed two teenagers who'd parked to neck near a creek in June, a fire that had consumed the north side of our town square in early July.

Had Daisy not arrived to weaken among the pews, Reverend Most may not ever have had a chance to deliver that sermon the following

Sunday; the seven men of the Board of Elders had marched up the aisle with the intention of demanding that the minister relinquish his collar right then and there. In the six months that the curly-headed twenty-nine-year-old minister had been at the Garden of Gethsemane Lutheran Church, the congregation had dropped by half. The church had hired Reverend Most to bring a young man's vigor to the pulpit, but all it had gotten was a young man's arrogance, and all he'd done was deny and stifle. He'd even, in one sermon, condemned the Miranda-and-Desiree books as "sick lullabies for our children, sung with the devil's tongue."

"My wife won't even come to church with me anymore," said Elder Dunleavy, his high-pitched, womanly voice scratched from years of puffing on cheap cigars every evening with a juice glass of happy-hour brandy. "She stays home to listen to the preachers on the AM radio."

Reverend Most, in T-shirt and jeans, just glanced down at the elders from the altar, his hands clutching both sides of the blond-wood pulpit. He stepped from the pulpit, down from the altar, and past the old men, even giving a few of them an impolite and superior shove. The elders' eyes followed after him, and that was when they saw a woman none of them had ever seen before weaving like a drunkard up the aisle.

A Lutheran church in Nebraska is typically a

place where any mad passion for Christ is politely concealed. Men and women recite the various creeds in hypnotic monotone; the hymns, pumped from wheezy organ pipes, are sung with no lilt or musicality. The members of the choirs not only don't dance, they don't sway. That's not to say no one is ever smacked hard with God's love or filled up to the eyeballs with the Holy Spirit, but when you are, you keep it to yourself. You don't leap to your feet, your tongue wrapping around the rapid gibberish of glossolalia; ministers don't slap your forehead to lift you, healed, from your wheelchair. There's never rending of garments or gnashing of teeth, and no one's ever dunked, wailing and baptized, into a country river.

So to have Daisy collapse against them, as battered and sweaty as a Baptist, her arms stretched out crucifixion-style, her eyes rolling back into her head, put some extra beats into the elderly hearts of the Board of Elders. Daisy's strangeness was charismatic; her blood on their hands was beautiful. And, for the first time, if they could admit it to themselves, the men felt their religion. They learned in that moment to love the circus that worship can be. Finally they could save someone from something terrible.

· 17 ·

As Daisy arrived in the chapel, Abby Most, the minister's wife, sat on pillows in the attic of the parish house, reading by the sunlight let in by a little half circle of window. She ate a pear, its juice sticky on her chin and fingers and spotting the pages of the Miranda-and-Desiree open in her lap: *The Mermaid Ghost*, the tenth book in the series.

Abby Most had listened to her husband's recent sermon on the corrupting influence of the Miranda-and-Desirees with guilt, her face burning bright pink. She'd leaned forward so her hair would drop and hide her blushing. Mrs. Bledsoe of her book club—for which they'd recently discussed the ninth book, *The Tattooed Spider*—had sat only a few pews up, and she'd glanced back to cast a cranky look at Abby. *The people of the Garden of Gethsemane Lutheran Church detest me,* Abby had thought, wringing her Kleenex to shreds in her fists, *even more than they detest the reverend,* because they could see, in Abby, a reasonable woman. *How can a wife stomach just sitting idly by?* they likely all wondered. But they simply didn't know Sammy in the late hours, all his virulent bedtime prayers whispered away into his folded hands, releasing his worry and anxiety over the sinful so he could sleep well and fight the devil again in the daylight. And, easefully and kindly, he'd hold Abby in his arms, becoming just as lost as everyone else, just as blind in the dark.

The Miranda-and-Desiree condemnation had proven his most notorious. We'd found it offensive and disrespectful, and a few of us had even left in the middle of it. In our town, we felt almost motherly toward the books, as many of us had been playing some part in printing them ever since Doc had signed the contract, back with the ninth in the series.

"Why isn't *our* factory printing the Bible?" the reverend had whined, indiscreetly, we'd thought. He'd held his own Bible up, shaking it evangelist-style. "This book, I happen to know, was printed in China. A godless country. The company that printed this book prints one million Bibles *every month*. If the world needs one million Bibles, then why can't we be the ones printing them? Think of the pride we could take in our work. Think how exciting it would be for our tiny little town to take the Bible-making industry away from the communists. And we wouldn't have to keep it secret. I say you should refuse to print the eleventh book. Strike. Sit down, stand up, whatever you have to do, but don't be a cog in the machinery of evil."

And it had seemed cruel to us that the minister should have chosen that particular Sunday to speak out against the Miranda-and-Desirees, against their séances and fallen angels, when the seventh book, one of the thickest, had just saved a life. When the first set of tornadoes had swept through our farmland the weekend before, a little girl had hidden beneath the kitchen table with her mother as the wind broke the windows of their ramshackle house. The girl had held the seventh book before her like a shield, protecting herself from the shattered glass while her mother's flesh was ripped to ribbons.

"Mrs. Most," the church secretary called up the attic stairs. "Are you up there, Mrs. Most?"

Abby paused for a moment, holding her breath, keeping still. But then she heard the creak of the stairs as the secretary climbed up anyway. "I'm here," Abby said. "Yes, yes, I'm here, I'm here, I'm here." She dropped the book into a box marked *Xmas*.

"You need to come to the chapel right away," the secretary said when she reached the top of the stairs. "There's a crisis."

"I'm up here because I have a migraine," Abby said. As she reached up to rub her temples, she hesitated, wondering if that gesture was just a touch too much. *The devil's in the details.* "I have to keep . . . well, I'm up here because I have to keep elevated."

"The elders are all in the church, but we need a woman right now," the secretary said.

"*You're* a woman," Abby said.

The secretary sighed. "Mrs. Most," she said. She shrugged her shoulders and took off her glasses to clean them with the cuff of her blouse. "You and your husband have run roughshod over this church since the second you darkened our doorstep. Now you have a chance to redeem yourself, and I'm trying to help you."

"Well, for goodness' sake, what's going on down there?"

"There's a woman . . . I don't know if she was beaten or if she was raped or if she was thrown out of a truck on the highway. She's just a mess. And she's not talking."

"What am I supposed to do about it?" Abby asked, but not in a snide way.

"Oh, Abby," the church secretary said, sighing some more. "You'll bring her here into the house. You'll clean her up, get her a robe and a brush. You'll make some tea. Put out those cookies I brought you yesterday. You'll be calm, and certain, and comforting."

"Okay," Abby said. "Okay. I'll be down in just a minute."

"No, not in a minute," the secretary said. "You'll come with me now." She held out her hand, and Abby took it, and the secretary led the minister's wife from the attic. She led her from the parish house, and into the church, and to the chapel, where the elders stepped aside to allow Mrs. Most to sit next to Daisy in the pew.

"What's your name, dear?" Abby asked. Daisy slouched, tired and docile, tracing a finger around a flower in the pattern of her dress. Abby put her hand on Daisy's wrist. "It's all right," Abby said. "You don't have to say anything at all." To the elders and to the reverend, this seemed exactly the right thing, this invitation to silence, and they were impressed by Mrs. Most's strategy. But it was Mrs. Most's own silence that she was negotiating. She was happy for Daisy to reveal nothing at all in her presence.

At first no sheriff, no doctor, was called. In the parish house, as Abby Most stood in front of the stove, arms folded, staring at the teakettle, dreading its whistle, the church secretary, in the other room, dabbed a cotton ball soaked with alcohol on the minor cuts from the leaves of the cornstalks.

The reverend's wife then led Daisy to the spare bedroom, where Daisy rested, the grandmotherly pillowcase—a baby-blue sateen—chilly against her cheek.

"Are you married?" Abby Most asked Daisy. Daisy shook her head. "Do you have any children?" No, again. "Do you live in town? Or nearby?" No. "On a farm?" No.

The reverend's wife touched at a string tied in a bracelet around Daisy's ankle. It was with that touch, that finger on that string, that everything came back in a horrid rush of clarity. Lenore, the night before, had tied that string there—the string had come loose from a ratty mop Daisy had used to wash the kitchen floor.

Lenore had been under the table, knotting Elvis's shoelaces together. Lenore, having grown bored by Elvis's visit and annoyed with all of Daisy's attention to him, had spent the day disappearing, scooting beneath tables, burrowing into closets.

So Lenore had tied the mop string around Daisy's ankle as Daisy had wiggled her foot around, gently kicking Lenore away. "Don't," Daisy had said, "that tickles." But Lenore had persisted.

And when the reverend's wife touched the string, it stung like a jolt of electric fence, and all the lack of feeling left Daisy's body, and the pain from running over the jagged furrows of the cornfield pulsed in the bottoms of her feet and worked up through the rest of her, returning the ache to her legs and her back. She didn't know what to do but cry. She curled up into a ball on the bed, buried her hands in her face, and wept and wailed, attracting the Board of Elders, who'd collected in the living room to worry as they'd stared into their cups of chamomile tea. They all slunk into the spare room like priests at a possession.

"Comfort her, Mrs. Most," the reverend told Abby. Her husband had never before called her

Mrs. Most, and on his tongue the name sounded like a scolding. Abby blushed. She hated his tone and the unspoken condescension of the old men in her house.

Abby scooted closer to Daisy on the bed and leaned over to whisper, "Tell me what to do." She took Daisy's hand, and Daisy gripped tightly. "Tell me what to do to help you, and I'll do it. I just need you to stop crying."

Daisy brought Abby's hand up to cover her own mouth. "I can't say it," it sounded like she said, in between sobs.

Abby Most turned to look back at the men in the room and in the hall. She fixed a mean squint on her husband, a man who'd at one time, on their first dates, their first months as boyfriend and girlfriend, been so careful not to scare her off. Back then, if he hadn't pleased her for even a moment, she could spend an afternoon not speaking and drop him into paroxysms of regret and apology.

"She says to get those old bastards out of here," she lied. The reverend opened his mouth but then closed it again. He turned to the elders, who'd already begun to leave the room. He then left too. He closed the door, making the knob latch as quietly as he could.

· *18* ·

I t's my fault," Daisy, still crying, told Abby. She sat on the bed with her knees up, rocking, and she twisted the string around and around her ankle.

"You can tell me about it," Abby said. "Or not. You don't *have* to tell me anything."

Daisy looked at Abby. "I have a little girl," Daisy said, slowly, as if confessing.

"Oh?" Abby said. "Oh?" she said again. She laughed a half laugh. "Then where is she? Your little girl?"

Daisy pulled her legs in tighter and pressed her forehead against her knees, whimpering. "I don't know," she said.

Abby had been imagining for Daisy nothing much more than some banal downward spiral of all-night liquor and squabbling. She'd pictured herself spending an afternoon braiding Daisy's hair, lending her a sensible dress, the husband showing up, sheepish, his very best cowboy hat held in his hands, and Daisy accepting his apology, but only after she'd made a handful of weepy, weak protestations.

But the suggestion of a lost girl hit Abby hard. Abby and the reverend had been trying for two years to have a child. And that child that wasn't, that might never be, took the blame, in Abby's imagination, for any minute too many of silence at dinner, or any terse word or spark of anxiety. *Comfort her, Mrs. Most.* That *Mrs. Most* at the end of his command—as if she were nothing more than a piece of him—certainly had as its source, at least partly, Abby's failure to get pregnant. Didn't it? Why else had things changed so much for them so quickly?

"Wait here," Abby told Daisy.

Abby walked down the hall and only halfway down the stairs. "We'll need to call the police," Abby said to the room of elders. And she stood there waiting, explaining nothing, until one of the men made a movement toward the phone in the kitchen. "Tell them there may be a missing child," Abby said then.

Abby returned to the bedroom, closing the door, and that was when Daisy first told the story she would tell again and again in the coming weeks— of Lenore under the table with the string from the mop, of Elvis on the farm, of his reading to them the counterfeit Miranda-and-Desiree he'd bought from the black market of Hong Kong, his airplane, the cider, the old pickup on blocks, his illicit baby talk, the new dress with the daisies on it, Lenore and Elvis nowhere in the morning.

And the Board of Elders, when told, chose to believe it all. They couldn't have worried more about Lenore if she'd been one of their own.

Part
FOUR

· 19 ·

Had the idea of Lenore simply occurred to Daisy as she'd languished in the parish house bedroom? Are there such psychological cases—childless women with delusions of motherhood? We'd heard of Munchausen syndrome by proxy, a pathology in which a mother, desperate for attention, wounds her child in some tender way (slight suffocation with a baby blanket, a teensy-weensy spoonful of kitchen cleanser) to have an excuse to visit a doctor or an emergency room and to bask in the attention we reserve for women with sickly babies. And, to be frank, it's a kind of insanity too many of us can understand. A doctor with an irresistible bedside manner, a nurse who hugs.

When my last husband—my second—died after three weeks in a hospital in Omaha, I couldn't bear to not go back to room 526. I desperately missed the nurses we'd loved, and I even missed the ones we hadn't liked nearly as much. I missed my husband's roommates (he'd had three in the three weeks there), and I missed his roommates' wives, and I even missed all their visitors. Polite, they'd respectfully looked past the partially drawn curtain to ask about my husband's condition, his progress, where we were from, what we'd done with our lives, when we might be going home. I loved the sardonic humor of my husband's nurses—the delight they took in temporary human fallibility. They were, to a person, unshaken by sickness, but not in a callous, cynical way. Their lack of sentiment was a beacon of hope—it was like they knew something we didn't, that there was no need to be morose, that they wouldn't bother with efforts of survival if survival was unlikely.

And so, two weeks after I buried my husband, I returned to the hospital in Omaha, checking into a nearby Holiday Inn. I spent most of one week on the hospital's first floor, in the cafeteria, the chapel, the florist. The corner coffee shop, with a wall of windows and a view of a memorial rose garden, served a pineapple-whip ice-cream cone that I'd been craving. I ate the cone and read a paperback I'd bought from the gift shop. I bought a tote bearing the hospital's logo, and a pair of slippers. I gossiped with the old-lady volunteers in their smocks, women who didn't know that my husband was dead and who kindly asked after his health. ("Good," was all I could bring myself to say—one simple word didn't seem like a psychotic lie.) I didn't dare go to my husband's old room. As much as I wanted to travel up in the brightly lit elevator with its carpet on the walls, I couldn't risk seeing someone alive in his bed, some survivor of something. And, of course, the nurses I'd loved would've spotted me, clucked their tongues with a mix of distress and sympathy, and sent me away. Our nurses belonged to other people now.

This went on for several days, until Doc found me out, and he and Tiff came to retrieve me. They walked up to me in the coffee shop as if they'd only happened by. They had liked the pineapple-whip cones too, so we spent a little while right there, pretending nothing was amiss. Doc finally let Tiff buy an overpriced yarn-haired rag doll she'd had her eye on in the gift shop throughout my husband's last weeks—Tiff was about seven at the time, Ivy having only just left her in Doc's care. "We can't buy it," he'd told her before; "we'd be depriving some sickly baby of it," and Tiff had learned to feel noble for simply not having the doll. But on this afternoon's return to the hospital, Doc slipped a ten-spot into Tiff's fist, as some kind of tribute to grief, perhaps. "I can't stand thinking of all those little girls walking by that ugly, pricey doll," he said, "and wanting it, and never getting it. The least we can do is get it out of the window." Then, later, "Cocktail hour," Doc said. "Let's go downtown for a martini," and with that, he and Tiff eased me out of the hospital, into the city, then onto the interstate, and home.

· 20 ·

No, wait. Wait. Before that, before we got in the pickup, we were in the back of it, in the bed of the pickup. We were dancing." Daisy put her hand to her head, tapping her fingers against her brow. "I'm sorry," she said. "I'm just not sure I'm remembering things right. Nothing's feeling right at all."

Doc and the sheriff sat at the kitchen table with her while I kept to the corner, inconspicuous but for the frequent creaking of the chair with each shift of my weight. I was a twin, I suppose, for the shrunken-apple-head doll in a bib-overall dress that had been propped there previously and now lay across my knees. I licked my thumb and wiped at the dust that had collected in its wrinkles and along its toothless smirk.

Daisy had changed from her daisy-print dress into a T-shirt and jeans. She sat with one foot up on her chair, her arms wrapped around her leg, as she fussed with the mop string still around her ankle. *The bottle of scotch on the kitchen table gleamed in a ray of sunlight, an amber ripple of reflection wavering on the tabletop,* Doc would write in his article, his first of many about the case. The bottle felt conspicuous, as did the glass next to it, and whenever anyone walked into the room, their eyes were drawn to the scotch. Was it as some sort of strategy that the sheriff and his deputies had left the bottle there?

Elvis, only a temporary presence in the house, had left evidence of himself everywhere. A disposable razor rested on the edge of a sink. A green bottle of aftershave sat on the windowsill in the tiny room in which he'd slept. There were stray hairs on the pillowcase, a man's shirt on a hanger in the closet, and, at the bottom of a garbage can, chewed-up toothpicks and a Band-Aid with a few little dots of blood. There was a bottle of beer on the nightstand, a cigarette butt at the bottom of it. And his airplane. The sheriff, in his investigation later that day, found a puddle of fuel in a patch of grass and a plane's tire tracks gouged into the earth. Weeds had been flattened and torn apart by the airplane's landing and takeoff.

Forensics could've gathered enough DNA to Frankenstein together a whole army of clones of Elvis, but Lenore remained ethereal. All Daisy had produced was a photograph, a Polaroid, taken by Elvis, she claimed. The picture was a blur, the girl in it hard to see. You could tell that the girl's hair was fine, and faint, and windblown, but you couldn't make out the set of her eyes or the shape of her chin, or whether she smiled or frowned for the picture, with lips thin or full.

Daisy told us she'd given birth eleven years ago, not in the hospital but in her own bedroom with the aid of a midwife and potent herb teas—hence no birth certificate, no hospital documents. The midwife's name was Mrs. Grey, Daisy explained, an old woman who lived in a little house on an island several miles up the Platte River. And there *was* a Mrs. Grey, we learned, and there *was* an island. But we were told by Mrs. Grey's daughter that the woman had long since died, felled by a swift cancer, dead only weeks after receiving the diagnosis from her doctor. Mrs. Grey, though cosmic in disposition, had kept detailed records, but the daughter had burned them all one autumn, file after file, in a brick oven behind the house, to ward off the chill when she had outdoor parties, her neo-hippie friends coming down from Grand Island with red wine and marijuana.

Soon enough, we discovered that the national reporters were extremely vulnerable to Lenore-inspired deception—the more absurd, it seemed, the more enticing. "Let me tell ya something," a fifteen-year-old boy told a news program. "Lenore wasn't so innocent. She and me used to sit in the ditch by her house and smoke cigarettes. She could smoke down more cigs than any other eleven-year-old girl I know. And it was beautiful, you know that? It was a thing of beauty to watch her smoke. When somebody really knows how to smoke, it's something to behold. I mean, she didn't do anything fancy— she didn't have to do . . . well, you know . . .

French inhales or nothing prissy like that. All she had to do was enjoy that cigarette, and she did. She took that smoke in deep, and she just blew it out slow, like she could care less how black her lungs were getting. I could watch that little girl smoke for days."

When dead birds showed up in the decoratively rusted cages so many had propped in their gardens that summer, people began to accuse Lenore. Some even claimed to have seen her slipping in and out of shadows with a leather satchel full of the corpses of swallows.

And within one week, when you Google-imaged Elvis, the first on the list was not the king of rock-and-roll but rather the police artist's sketch of Lenore's presumed abductor. The sketch artist, a local, had been previously criticized for his elaborate portraits, his artistry overwhelming his work, creating images so detailed that all you remembered was the picture, not what lowly criminal the picture might represent. For Elvis, he practically stripped the man of all individuality, creating a blank slate we could endow with any number of distinguishing marks. We could see that face in nearly every man we met, and the sketch provoked all sorts of erroneous sightings.

And our paper, the County Paragraph, conspired with our community, dignifying every slim possibility by weighing its potential for fact. Even the slightest bit of scrutiny managed to give the most unlikely scuttlebutt legs and longevity. People everywhere wanted news of Lenore directly from us—we gained subscribers from across the country and around the world, even in cities where they didn't speak English. People trusted us for our folksiness—we seemed too good-hearted to traffic in lies. It was an absurd notion, of course; small towns historically have thrived on weaving tall tales—villages are easily taken in by sideshow promise and religious ecstasy. A potato with the profile of Christ bleeds from an eye, and the farmer who dug it up will go to his grave defending its holy implications.

Though, as you already know, I never published Lenore's obituary, my obituaries nonetheless developed what could only be called a cult following. People, no matter how far away, seemed to love to read about our local dead—they loved taking measure of such tiny lives and loved to think of me as a little old lady with a dark passion. They could just picture me in veils and ribbons and widow's weeds, high on hemlock tea, it always winter out my window, my skeleton's fingers rattling at my typewriter, writing my death sentences. I paraded before them a necropolis of folks who might've been worth their knowing: Mrs. Lacey Norris, the hospital volunteer who crocheted caps for years and years of newborns, who went ass-over-elbows down a long flight of stairs; Mr. Benjamin Lake, inventor of an innovative coyote trap, whose night sweats proved more dire than just the consequence of too many quilts on the bed; Mrs. Helen Law, glassblower, smoke inhalation; Mr. Weston Ansley, insurance, natural causes; Mrs. Geraldine Speck, Autoharp enthusiast, bone disease; Mr. E. A. West, organist, lungs; Mr. Nelson Barnet, grocer, kidneys; Miss Ellen Maxwell, jeweler, blood.

And I've been condemned for having this career at all; I've been addressed, in letters, as Morticia and Vampira and Queen of the Dead. I've been accused of taking fiendish delight in mortality, capitalizing on loss.

Who will write my obituary, and what will it say? How could it possibly be anything but superficial and inadequate? Don't I deserve, for having written thousands of obituaries, to have one that's better than any of those thousands I've written? Is it so much to want the last sentence of my obit to be written by someone of genius? I want my obituary to win awards, to be published in textbooks. I want future obituary writers to say, "I knew I wanted to be an obit writer when I read so-and-so's obit of S Myles." And when the writer of my obituary dies, I want her obituary to mention mine.

· 21 ·

With Lenore's disappearance, Doc saw an opportunity for redemption, though he may not have thought of it in that way, exactly. In that terrible summer, there'd been not just tornadoes but fires as well. Sparklers, those harmless sticks kids lit and twisted around in front of themselves, writing their names in sputtering trails of silver light, had become the latest dangerous experiment—duct-tape hundreds of them together and you could blow things to smithereens, for amusement. A one-hundred-year-old building, a cornerstone of the historic town square, castle-like with cupolas and arches and wrought-iron spikes, had gone up in flames a few days before the fourth of July, a ragtag gang of twelve-year-olds having set off a sparkler bomb in the alley.

There was a desperate need in the community to place blame. God took some of that blame, but not all that he deserved. Some of it went to my grandson, and our newspaper, as if we rewarded bad weather and bad behavior by writing about them.

But no one could stop learning about Lenore. And we were mistrustful of the national news. The magazine and TV writers overindulged their fascination with the gothic, and we simply didn't recognize ourselves in their reports. So our own people turned to the County Paragraph for the stories we wanted to be told, and Doc quickly earned a new respect. He became, in his charmingly affected linen suits and neckties and retro fedoras of various patterns, our Stage Manager, our Music Man. Our one-man Greek chorus. He was also the character you root for in a movie—we'd all been longing for him to step out of his father's shadow and make something of that newspaper again.

And he had to do so while our own family became more and more unfamiliar to us. Despite the fact that Ivy had been away from Tiff for years, her sudden reappearance made Doc feel like a bad parent. Ivy was everywhere now, almost always among us, and though she never said much, nursing one glass of red wine through a whole evening, her silence felt condemning. Ivy always looked puzzled by the family's habits— when we ate, what we ate, when we went to bed, what we wore to bed. Our terms of endearment and other gestures of affection all came under scrutiny just by virtue of having a stranger among us. Ivy would furrow her brow at the drop of a hat, and Doc would instantly question his own judgment.

"What?" Doc would sometimes say at the sight of Ivy's accusatory squint.

"Nothing," she'd say. "I didn't say anything."

Tiff was finally eating again, at least, though not without some coaxing. Doc, though busy with the newspaper, made it a point to join us every evening for supper, sometimes arriving after I'd served the salad and having to leave before I served dessert, but his presence was to assure Tiff that she couldn't anymore starve herself away unwatched.

Things overall seemed to be going fairly well, all of our tempers in accord with Tiff's appetite. Nonetheless, there was *a night that everything changed,* you might say, if you were feeling particularly dramatic, and who in our town wasn't in those days? We were finishing up our pot roast when Ivy said, "Tiff, are you done eating?" Tiff, of course, was. "Would you go up to your room, please? I'd like to talk to your uncle about some things. Before he has to rush off again."

Tiff dropped her jaw and clucked her tongue. Usually that was her expression of mock teenage-y disgust, but this time it was authentic. She looked to Doc. "Why do I have to go to my room? I don't have to go to my room, do I?"

Doc took a deep breath. "Ummm," he muttered, then looked at me. I straightened up in my chair and stroked my chin.

"Well, Ivy," I said, "we don't really do that here. I mean, we've never sent Tiff to her room before. Have we?" I looked at Doc.

"No, we kind of don't do that," Doc said, still looking at me, nodding. "We've just always talked about things in front of her. We've always liked to be open about things."

Ivy said nothing more until we both turned to look at her. She was smiling, but not unkindly. "I know," she said. "I'm just hoping that, just this once, Tiff might leave us alone for a few minutes. She doesn't have to go to her room, I understand that. If you don't do that, we shouldn't do that, we shouldn't ask her to go to her room. But I don't think it's too much to ask for a little privacy. Privacy isn't a terrible thing. So if Tiff doesn't want to go to her room, fine. Maybe *we* can go to *your* room," she gestured toward Doc with her butter knife, then pointed the knife toward the window, "or across the street to Granny's house."

"Maybe let's just not make it such a big deal," Tiff said, blessedly coming to everyone's rescue. "I'll go to my room. Can I go on the Internet, at least?"

We all said yes.

After Tiff left the table, Ivy lifted her wineglass. "Fill 'er up, please?" she said to Doc, and he poured her some more. "So, tell me," she said, "what is Madame, um, is it *Yamasaki's* Cabinet?"

"Madame Sakaguchi's Japanese Cabinet, you probably mean?"

"Probably," Ivy said.

"It's a magic act."

"It's a magic act," she said. "What does it entail, exactly?"

"Well, it's a cabinet, a beautiful red lacquer cabinet, with some trick doors."

"And you have one, right?"

"Ivy," Doc said, rubbing one of his eyes with his thumb, "can we . . . what are you . . . ?"

"I'm just asking you questions," Ivy said. "I'm not trying to be coy and obnoxious. I'm just asking because I don't know. I don't speak the family language, Doc. I don't know the codes, I don't know the references, I don't know all the cute little words for things that you've all got. Yes, I've been gone for a long time, and yes, I should be punished unrelentingly for that, but—"

"I'm not saying that," Doc said.

"Well, whatever." Her *whatever,* however, was sharp with irritation. She rolled her eyes and stabbed at her potato skin with her fork.

"Madame Sakaguchi's Japanese Cabinet, yes, I've got one," he said. "Tiff and I drove to Iowa City, probably, I don't know, three years ago, was it?" He looked at me, but I'd sunk down into the chair, my hand covering most of my face, preferring the invisibility I'd mastered as a shy little girl. "It was on an auction bill. I paid too much for it because I was bidding against an interior designer who wanted it for some Asian decor she was doing someplace."

"And how does it work, exactly, if I can ask without you flipping out on me?"

"Why don't I show you?" he said with a

sarcastic sweep of his arms in the direction of the kitchen. "It's in the garage."

Ivy simply stood, lifted her glass, and walked toward the kitchen. Every night at dinner, Ivy at his table, Doc had been respectful and accommodating. He'd never lectured her, never staked any claims on Tiff's future. And now, having asked Tiff to leave the room, Ivy dared to assume authority in his house. I was a touch miffed myself at this cryptic line of questioning. Behind her back, Doc mouthed the words *Oh, my God* at me, and I mouthed back *I know, I know,* but I did so while furrowing my brow, flinching a little, attempting to articulate that, though Ivy was clearly being difficult, he should be gentle with her for Tiff's sake. He seemed to pick up on all that, and he nodded and took my wineglass from me for a sip.

After we'd passed through the kitchen and into the garage, Doc lifted a blue sheet from the cabinet in the corner with a showy "Voilà." It truly was a beautiful piece, its fiery-nosed dragon painted in gold leaf, its door lined with mother-of-pearl.

"It's a classic trick," Doc said, "though kind of primitive. The girl gets in, the magician shuts the door, presto change-o, the magician opens the door, the girl's gone, but she's not gone because she's hiding down here," and Doc knocked his knuckles at the bottom of the cabinet. "These bottom legs are supposed to have a slanted mirror between them, to reflect the carpet or whatever and kind of give the illusion that there's not a hiding place down there, but the mirror had broken off, and I've never replaced it."

"And you and Tiff do this act sometimes," Ivy said.

Doc sighed and started rubbing his eye again. "What is it, Ivy? You disapprove of Tiff taking part in a magic act? You think it's Satanic, I suppose?"

Ivy sighed herself and sat on the bumper of the car. She took a drink of wine. "Tiff told me in confidence, so I shouldn't even be telling you this at all, but I'm telling you because I think you'd want to know, even though you'll probably run right upstairs and tell her that I told you, because you're all so *open* with each other, but she told me that the last time you did the act with the cabinet, she couldn't fit in the bottom, and the act was ruined."

"It wasn't ruined," Doc said.

"It wasn't ruined," I said.

"We made a joke of it. That's part of our act. Comedy's always been part of our act. Tiff and I aren't talented magicians, so we ham it up, and people love it. When she got stuck, it was cute, it was really cute. We were at a nursing home, for God's sake. They ate it up. They thought it was adorable."

"But you haven't done the act since, right?" Ivy said.

"Well, no, but we haven't really had many gigs since," he said.

"Tiff told me that she couldn't fit into the cabinet anymore because she's gotten too fat, and that's why you don't do the act anymore, and that's why she stopped eating. She wishes she could still fit in the box."

Doc and I looked at each other, our mouths open, about to offer some sort of defense, some sunny alternative to the grim truth Ivy had just revealed, but then we shut our mouths and kept quiet. We all kept quiet, in the garage, drinking our wine, looking at the once coveted Madame Sakaguchi's Japanese Cabinet in all its rapidly fading glory.

· 22 ·

Of course, Lenore became increasingly difficult to believe in, even for the believers. And those of us who turned skeptical found ourselves wishing Daisy had at least done a better job of inventing a child. She could've filled the room with stuffed animals, stuck puffy stickers to the headboard of her bed. She could've left on the nightstand a half-eaten licorice whip or a jawbreaker partly licked away. Daisy could've put an unfinished game of Clue on the kitchen table and placed muddy sneakers on the welcome mat. We all theorized how *we* would've done it, how expertly we could've kept people chasing shadows for years.

Nonetheless, the mile up to the farm became riddled with pilgrims—station wagons and minivans were parked along the side of the road, and people filled the ditches with plastic memorial wreaths and framed photographs and stuffed animals, tributes to Lenore and to other lost children. Among the clutter were even childhood pictures taken in the 1950s, teens gone so long they'd long since grown old somewhere else.

These out-of-towners ate in our restaurants, bought gas at our stations, booked up our motels, and frequented our shops, and though an old-fashioned country skepticism made us anxious for an easy, obvious truth, we knew better than to dismiss Daisy as a fraud. To declare Lenore nonexistent would be to bite the hand that fed us. For the sake of a business-like practicality, we were determined to be impractical—fanciful, even. We even indulged unorthodox investigators: the psychics, the mind readers, the hypnotists, shipped in by news networks from as far away as Berlin. On TV, the supernaturalists stood among patches of overgrown weeds on the farm, speaking with certainty about their intuitions.

One afternoon, a woman named Jane David came to town, a woman who read cracks in mirrors the way others read bumps on heads or the scatter of wet tea leaves. The practice was not evolved from French witchcraft or tribal shamanism but born of fiction, derived from the Miranda-and-Desiree books themselves, the fourth book, *The Dead Weights of the Doll's Head*. A mystic in the novel made all her predictions based on how a mirror broke. In her coach, which was tugged through towns by a team of two donkeys, the mystic kept all the drawers in her vanity filled with hand mirrors. She presented one to Miranda, who paid a one-dollar fee, and Miranda looked into it for a full minute, then slapped the mirror against a brick. The mystic ran her finger along the resulting crack, her eyes closed, and from the crooked path of the break she envisioned the girl's bleak future.

In the many years since the fourth book, the reading of broken mirrors had taken shape—it had a name *(glancing)* and a professional association (AGAzE: American Glancing Association of Entrepreneurs) and even its own Dummies' guide. Of all the glancing specialists, Jane David was the most famous, having had a short-lived reality show on the Discovery Channel in which she'd traveled the world to read broken mirrors—she read existing cracks and cracks newly made. She read cracks in mirrors in houses purported to be haunted, mirrors on movie sets, in the telescopes of stargazers.

Jane David waived her enormous fee in order to conduct a private consultation at the Crippled Eighty.

"I believe you," Jane told Daisy upon arriving, before Daisy even spoke a word. Jane always talked quickly, always fussing with an unkempt curl or two. She wore a simple white blouse and a simple tan skirt and what looked to be pearlescent ballerina slippers. "Lenore is an enigma," she told Daisy. "She's an Alice having fallen into the Looking Glass, now, isn't she? We just have to reach in and yank her on out." Jane David mimicked reaching into something and yanking something out, making her hand into a fist and bringing it to her chest. Her secretary lit a cigarette, then poked it in between the fingers of that fist. "You don't mind if I smoke," Jane David said, looking into Daisy's eyes as if hypnotizing her.

First Jane David examined the mirrors in the house, finding whatever cracks she could. "Da Vinci wrote in some of his notebooks backward," Jane David mumbled, her head back, her eyes closed, her fingers pressed against a crack that snaked along a corner of a mirror in a gilt frame that hung in a hallway. "I've held those journals in my hands," she said. "I held the pages up to a mirror, and when I read them, I knew that the Mona Lisa was a woman he'd fallen in love with." She opened her eyes, looked at Daisy, and reached out. "Touch the hand that touched Da Vinci's papers," she said.

Daisy hesitantly, gently, placed her hand in Jane David's. For a moment, Jane and Daisy held hands, until Jane snapped her hand back as if Daisy's had suddenly grown hot.

Out in Lenore's garden, Jane David's secretary tossed mirrors onto the hard dirt to break. Jane squatted next to the mirrors. She stroked her chin and shook her head. When she dropped her cigarette and stubbed it out with the toe of her slipper, we noticed that her slippers were speckled with the dots and holes of cigarette burns.

"You'll hear from me," she told Daisy. Jane David, all business, fled the farm, twisting her hair, and later that day a young boy on a bicycle rode up to Daisy's front door. He handed her a letter from Jane David.

"I wish I could tell a lie," the letter began, "but never before have I felt so powerful a certainty. I would not be doing you a courtesy, Daisy, if I told you that I thought your daughter still lived. She has died, and she has died violently. To settle her soul, you must release her. Find a coffin, a little white one, put a doll in it if you must, but bury it, say a prayer over it, have her name carved into a gravestone. End everything. Let her spirit leave that decrepit farm."

Daisy cried. She dropped the letter to the floor of the front porch, and she went into the house.

We could hear her crying, and hear the wailing rise and echo, and we didn't know if she'd ever stop. Her hiding behind the ratty drapes of the house of the Crippled Eighty served both her devotees and her detractors. *She's devastated,* some said, while others said, *She can no longer sustain the lie.*

Part
FIVE

· 23 ·

In the months before the publication of the eleventh book, the date of release set for mid-December, the highly secretive author, Wilton Muscatine, had revealed only a title: the novel was to be called *The Coffins of Little Hope*. Could this mean that Miranda and Desiree would finally find their mother, who they'd long believed to be an undertaker's widow in the village of Cranberry Bog? Was Little Hope a person? Or only a condition?

Muscatine never made appearances, never gave interviews; children, even the healthy ones, pained him too much, not from annoyance but from the vulnerabilities so evident—from their runny noses and tangled knots of dirty hair to their skinned knees and mouthfuls of lost baby teeth. He himself had grown up in foster homes, oversensitive, often paddled for daydreaming. To Muscatine, childhood was a gothic keep; like a princess in a tower, he'd longed for rescue.

How could I know such intimacies about such an unknowable man? I know because, in those days of Lenore, he wrote me letters.

"It's very surprising to look forward to the mail again," I told Tiff over breakfast one morning in my kitchen. She'd flipped together some chocolate-chip pancakes, mostly so she could wear the ruffled apron, of an impractical blue silk, I'd bought her for her home economics class. "It's like getting messages in bottles."

I didn't tell Tiff that the letters were from Muscatine. When I received the first fan letter he sent to me, I suspected fraud. Why would he write to *me?* He'd written on the white side of a square of Miranda-and-Desiree holiday gift wrap that featured illustrations from the sixth book, Muscatine's Christmas-themed novel, the one in which Miranda and Desiree fall into a crack in the frozen lake and meet watery phantoms in long, flowing scarves skating figure eights across the underside of the lake's layer of ice. *Forgive the lack of proper notepaper,* he wrote, *but I have reams upon reams of this god-awful stuff. All the paper wasted on me keeps me up at night. My books, so far, have killed eight million trees.*

"Are they love letters, Essie?" Tiff asked.

"No," I said.

I'm not sure I've ever received a love letter in my life. My few lovers, when alive, had always been within my proximity.

· 24 ·

Doc continued to regularly publish that photo of Lenore on the front page, that same abstract snapshot that revealed practically nothing week after week, throughout September and

October, the image sharp in our memories even as it dissolved before our eyes, the girl vanishing little by little the closer we looked at her. Doc ran the photo alongside articles reporting even the slightest changes in the case, of which there were few. "The Mystery of Lenore Still Unsolved" read one dreary headline. The town went back to criticizing Doc. Time to move on, read their letters to the editor. *We're much more than just that missing girl.* But I knew, and Doc knew, that that was not what the town really wanted. Even their protestations seemed meant, consciously or not, to keep Lenore alive. Though the townspeople did not actively contrive together, didn't gather, didn't vote on the subject of Daisy's claims, we recognized our need for notoriety.

Even when Doc composed his own editorials, about other things entirely, his metaphors always seemed to lean in Lenore's direction. "As some of you know," he wrote in a mid-October edition of "Another Think Coming," his weekly column, "I've had, for the last few years, an amateur magic act. And as some of you have witnessed, I'm not very good at it. To the great relief of my niece, Tiffany, who serves as my lovely assistant, I don't strap her to a spinning wheel and throw meat cleavers at her. The results would be unhygienic, I suspect. And though, together, we've enjoyed our clumsy approximations of creaky tricks, I worry my girl is outgrowing not just the little boxes she tucks herself into but also our time together. She has turned 13, and spending Sunday afternoons at old-folks' homes with her eccentric uncle, pulling rabbits out of hats, is likely growing old hat, lickety-split. So, long story short . . . *For sale: one Madame Sakaguchi's Japanese Cabinet, slightly shopworn, with a trapdoor and hidden compartment.* It would make a great wardrobe, or maybe you could add some shelves and turn it into a bar. But, if you're like me, making kids disappear, even for the sake of illusion, isn't feeling much like entertainment these days."

Over the years in his weekly editorials Doc had, with mixed success, affected his father's fatherly patter. Doc's father, in his classic hard-act-to-follow fashion, had been the beloved narrator of our every tale. Doc had respectfully kept the title of Josiah's column, but the patronizing tone, even one so cherished, had seemed to him no longer relevant. He'd immediately done away with some of the folksier aspects, such as the collective first person *(after we ate up our heaping slice of humble pie, we asked the missus if she could at least serve it up á la mode next time)* and the cast of down-home archetypes: the missus, sonny-boy, little sis, granny. I don't think people had been as distressed about Doc's revisions as they'd been about what they'd represented: yet another simple thing lost to antiquity.

· 25 ·

Tiff and Ivy bleached their hair a matching platinum blond on the afternoon of the auditions for *Missing in America*, the popular TV documentary series. The tryouts, held in the high school's gymnasium, were for the dramatizations to be filmed for a Lenore-based episode. *Missing in America* traveled across the country, gathering interviews and news footage, to bring attention to recent abductions—the company's short caravan of a few RVs had driven up from Oklahoma, where it had filmed an episode about a pierced-lipped teenybopper believed snatched by a carny who'd operated the Screaming Mimi at the state fair.

Ivy and Tiff hoped for the parts of Daisy and Lenore, though Daisy's hair, in reality, wasn't platinum. Ivy clearly just wanted to indulge in a mother-daughter dye job. I waited for them in a red-vinyl booth down the street at the café, having sneaked in my own vodka cocktail, sipping from the thermos lid as I wrote a letter to Muscatine. *When you're old,* I wrote, *you begin to feel like something worse than useless. You become a distressing and vivid reminder that there's no exit of grace and beauty.*

Even when not in the act of writing Muscatine a letter, I was often composing one in my mind, situating the words just so, plunking one here, then one there, gauging how to sound worthy of his regard. Whereas Muscatine had written on whatever paper was near at hand, I'd had stationery printed, a thick stock of a light violet hue, *S Myles* embossed at the top. In the letters I'd received, he'd spoken mostly of his addiction to the County Paragraph (mailed weekly to his home in Brooklyn, New York). *I was sent over the moon by your obit for Jolene Watkins,* he'd written in his first letter, *and her devastating collection of dollys with crochet gowns concealing rolls of toilet paper. Oh to visit that collection of gawd-awful dawls!*

The café was packed with Daisys and Lenores—some little girls with hair bleached a shocking-white shade of corn silk, others bewigged, others naturally blond. At the counter sat the town's swarthiest—the men fancying themselves worthy of the role of the dangerously magnetic Elvis, most of them affecting the famous police sketch's interpretation, with forelocks and cowlicks, that mussed look of men too comfortable in bed.

"There should be some auditions for somebody to play me, don't you think?" Doc said, scooting in across the table from me, having gone to the counter for a slice of pumpkin pie. "I've been very involved." And he'd certainly dressed for the part that afternoon, his getup particularly colorful despite the bone-white linen of his suit—his buttonhole sported a silk orchid, a knotted watch chain dangled in a loop from a vest pocket, his socks were argyle. "What's with the Cheshire-cat grin?" he said.

"I don't have a Cheshire-cat grin," I said. "I'm not even showing teeth. A Cheshire-cat grin is a big, wide-mouthed, full-of-teeth grin. I think you mean I look like the cat that ate the canary. That's the grin you're thinking of." My correspondence I kept secret. The man writing to me as Muscatine might not have been Muscatine at all. As far as I knew, my pen pal could have been an imposter. Even *that* I found tantalizing, the possibility of some stranger compelled to deceive me. But I didn't want my letter-writing, and my letter-writer, to be speculation for anyone at all.

"You're right," he said, sighing, taking my correction a bit too much to heart, it seemed. "I'm full of mistakes, always. Maybe I'll be ruined."

"Ruined by what?" I said, reaching across to pinch his arm.

"For telling Daisy's story," he said.

"You won't be ruined," I said. For years I'd felt pangs of regret, and pangs of guilt for that regret, that Doc was so ill-suited for the family business. But there was no denying he'd finally found his voice. The people in our county—having been run ragged by debt and bankers and biblically bad weather for years—had come to need not just

Daisy and Lenore but also Doc's gracious portrait of them.

Doc dropped a quarter into the tabletop jukebox and selected a song I recognized not at all—it could've been old, it could've been new. But I knew for certain that the jukebox itself, with its neon flicker, and all the other little jukeboxes tucked into the café's booths, were recent additions. The café had been slinging hash at farmers since the 1940s but had never before had tabletop jukeboxes. They were a nod toward a nostalgia for a time that never was.

Other main streets in little towns in the state were going through costly renovations to look old-fashioned. Those towns installed streetlamps with elegant frosted globes and wrought-iron hooks from which they hung pots of begonias, and they mounted their police on Clydesdales. They reopened their opera houses for amateur productions of melodramas and olios. They installed soda fountains in hardware stores and subsidized used-book stores and candy shops for the sake of charm. But *our* town . . . we were much too late to pursue our history—too many other communities around us had beaten us to it, and we were too far off the interstate for tourists to be lured by a quick stop-off for saltwater taffy and sips of local wines.

In the town of Lemontree (which all the locals pronounced not "lemon tree" but rather "la-*mawn-*

tree"), in the next county over, benefactors were buying up all the properties, restoring them, filling them with antiquities, as if they were carving Pompeii from its ashes. Lemontree had been the home of Myrtle Kingsley Fitch, the writer. There was the bank with its vault (the inspiration for Myrtle's short story "The Bank Vault") and an opera house where Myrtle had danced in recitals as a girl. The grocery store was now a museum, the post office a gallery of Western art, the haberdashery a concert hall due to its quirky acoustics. For years, the bountiful Myrtle Kingsley Fitch Foundation had been saving that dying rural town by killing it, inch by inch, and casting it in amber.

"You feel a little fatherly toward Lenore," I suggested. But we all did, whether we believed in her or not. Our collective fear for Lenore, for Daisy, put some fight in us. The legend of Lenore, if carefully composed, would save our town from a quaint decline into barbershop quartets and taxpayer-supported ice-cream parlors.

"Tiff was seven? Wasn't she? When Ivy left?" Doc said. He fiddled with a matchbook, twisting a few matches into a redheaded stick figure. "Tiff has missed Ivy every day of her life since, and every day of her life she's expected Ivy to just show up again. And now here she is. She showed up. So now everything's good, right? Back to normal?" Doc took a sip from my thermos lid, smacked his lips, and turned up his nose. "Needs a little soda pop or something," he said. It was a sour brew I'd concocted myself with a glass urn, a few bottles of the grocery store's cheapest vodka, and the cherries I'd plucked in June from the Nanking bush at my kitchen window. I'd planted the bush years before because the tart bite of the cherries reminded me of one fine summer of my first widowhood.

"Did I ever tell you how I never loved your grandfather?" I said. I'd married him because my grandmother, a classic German-Russian battle-ax, had wanted me to. And it was her I'd blamed when he'd widowed me, leaving me alone with our little boy. I have few warm feelings for cold old Theodore with the fatally and metaphorically weak heart, who, at this late point, seems barely to have ever happened to me at all. It was my *second* husband who I'd loved, though he and I had met so late in his life, we'd had only ten years together.

"Yes," Doc said. "Many times. It makes you feel rebellious to say it."

"Did I ever tell you that I had a love affair three months after his death?"

Doc looked at me. Of course I hadn't told him. But it was time that he got to know me. My sister, nearly ninety, rattled off so much nonsense as she paced the halls of her nursing home that no one knew what was truth and what was symptomatic of her *dementia*—that poetic word for a departing, psychedelic brain. Married and divorced five times, Lydia had had a long life of peril and indulgence, and her nurses all secretly wanted to believe her every breath of scandal.

"I was only thirty but looked old for my age," I told Doc. "I had bags under my eyes and puffy purple lips. That, with the dead husband and the twelve-year-old orphan, made me just damaged enough to be appealing to the mean son of a bitch."

That son of a bitch had been much on my mind lately, which was the reason I'd spent the afternoon sipping cherry vodka. The man had had in his yard a cherry bush, every year letting the fruit rot and fall to the ground. One evening we'd drunk martinis while sitting in the grass, me in my best dress, and I'd identified the plant for him, assuring him that the cherries weren't poisonous. I'd taken a toothpick from his front pocket and poked some of the cherries, dropped them into my glass of vodka, and toasted suicide before taking a gulp and laughing. I'd leaned back on my elbow, at the edge of a pond with a few black fish among its gold ones, and as I'd watched one of the fish nibble on the end of a dried leaf floating on the surface of the water, I'd begun to doubt my own knowledge of deadly horticulture. All the deaths by poison I'd ever explained in my years of obit-writing had come tumbling back into my brain:

nervous Mrs. Peamont with her hexagonal blue bottle, with its skull-and-crossbones paper label, clutched in her fist; slow Charlie St. James eating daffodil bulbs in the greenhouse. But what a way to go, I had decided, taking another sip of my drink—death by cherries in a summer cocktail during a near-illicit rendezvous.

Aw, don't crumble, Cookie, my cruel lover had told me weeks later as I'd wept, in only my slip, after a noontime roll. He'd kept having to knot and re-knot his necktie to get it to hang precisely at his belt buckle. *It's just over, that's all. Don't let something like this get to you. You're smarter than that, pretty girl. Don't turn this into some romantic collapse. It's not worth it, trust me.* But even as he'd said it all, with a pitying smile he'd watched in the vanity mirror, I'd known he was only saying it to wound me forever, to be the man who broke my heart irreparably.

"Some man was terrible to you?" Doc said. The kid seemed to be getting tears in his eyes.

"Oh, boy, do I already regret bringing it up," I said, tapping Doc's hand with the end of my pencil. "Forget I said anything. It was six weeks out of my life. I don't want to talk about it. I barely remember a minute of it." And why *had* I told him? I blamed my pen pal. I'd had only a few weeks of exchanging letters with Muscatine, but no sooner would I send off a letter than I'd receive one. And his fame, certainly, played a part in my being so beguiled. And maybe his wealth. All the things that could've distracted me at thirty distracted me now.

And Muscatine's distraction was Lenore. Though he couldn't possibly fret about every pitiful and pitiable child who nagged at his sympathies, he found himself curious about Daisy and her daughter, and he subscribed to our newspaper, and he learned who we were, and he took to our stories, to our little lives, like a native, a prodigal son yet to return.

"Why do you make us live here in the middle of nowhere?" Tiff asked Doc, joining us in the booth. Her chiding was affectionate, and she wrapped her arms around him. "If we lived in Hollywood, I could be a child star." Tiff wore an old dress of mine, one she'd found in the back of a basement closet, something from the 1970s that had turned, so quickly, vintage. It had been one of those pieces of clothing you end up keeping for years and years, its price tags still on it, because you think you might still someday wear it, despite its having always looked better on the hanger. Tiff had discovered it in her effort to cultivate an eccentricity, ignored its mothball stink, and tailored it, loving its old-lady sofa-pattern print of cut-open pomegranates.

"You do have your mother's hambone," Doc said. Ivy, who sat next to me, reached across the table to slug him in the shoulder, playful but hard, and we all realized with a start that that was the first chummy gesture she'd made toward her brother since her return from Paris.

"Maybe Daisy *sold* Lenore," Doc said, running his fingers through the tangled, rat's-nest ends of Tiff's bleached hair. "Or gave her away. Then destroyed all of Lenore's stuff. Then maybe she regretted it, but she can't tell the whole truth."

Tiff reached back to slap his hand away. "Ouch, you're pulling," she said. But then he started doing it again, and she let him.

I couldn't help but notice Ivy watching Doc and Tiff as she fussed with the ends of her own bleached hair.

We picked up some fried chicken and slaw from Cluck's on the way home and ate in front of the TV at Doc's. Tiff gnawed on three legs of chicken. Halloween was only a few weeks away, and one of the cable stations played horror movies, back to back, and we all stayed up, getting loopier with each late hour. After midnight, the room lit only by a black-and-white daughters-of-Dracula flick, the four of us drowsy but anxious about the milky-skinned neck of a Transylvanian nun, Ivy suddenly leaped to her feet, her hands in claws, and moaned a strangled cry that made us jump. Ivy laughed big at our fright, clutching her gut.

"That's mean!" Tiff said, but five minutes later, she did the same thing, startling us just as effectively as Ivy had, with the exact same sudden, strangled cry. We were easy victims, it seemed.

"I don't have a young heart, children," I said. But the scare tactics continued for days—Ivy, to her delight, had established a new family tradition. It had become our "thing." Even daylight held the possibility of someone lunging from around a corner with a maniac's howl. We'd been no strangers to tension in Doc's house since Ivy's return, but now the house was haunted with a madcap threat.

· 26 ·

By the end of October, Daisy consented to venture forth from the Crippled Eighty, to come back out of hiding, accepting invitations to appear at late-fall revivals in tents, held at all hours in the countryside, the farmers exhausted and dirty from harvest, needing ritual, needing communion with the earth and the night sky, desperate to connect with the land they ravaged. The moon, all that autumn, cast a glow the color of bourbon, silhouetting bats and blackbirds against the sky, sticking the wicked in the Halloween witches. Daisy often rambled on and on in her worship, in a manner that was taken for passion.

"People are so proud of themselves," Daisy said when called to the pulpit by Rev. Sammy Most. "They think they're smarter than God. And they kind of are, because you know what? God's a child. He's not an old man with a gray beard. He's a child, and he acts like a child. But the beauty of everything is because he sees everything with a child's eyes. The cobwebs and how they sparkle. The veins of a leaf. The segments of an ant. When it's not winter, God's in everything, even in the way a flower wilts or drops its petals. People are so proud of themselves because they think they're the ones that invented beauty. They think they invented beauty by simply recognizing it and calling it beauty. Through their genius, the world is beautiful. How would that make you feel if you were God?"

God had punished Daisy, she explained to the parishioners. As a tornado had ripped through the Crippled Eighty the previous May, she'd held Lenore tight in her arms. She had felt the wind pulling hard at them both, threatening to buckle their knees and whip them away. They'd watched the little garden shed lift from its foundation, the thin boards of its walls separating, fanning out like a hand of cards. They'd heard the creak of bending steel echoing. "'God's throwing a tantrum,' I told Lenore," Daisy said to the congregants in the tent. "'God's spoiled rotten.' But it was beautiful, there, then, clutching my daughter tight in my arms, refusing to let God suck her into his fit of violent hatred. *You can't,* I thought. *You can't do nothing to us.*"

Daisy's oddball gospels built her an entourage of hangers-on, all of whom had seen better days. These reformed drunks and repentant wife-beaters, and the wives they'd stopped beating, attended to Daisy, hoping for their heretofore indifferent God to witness their proximity to Daisy's sainthood and suffering. They cooked her lunches and dinners, bubbled her hot baths, soaped her back and washed her hair. They wrote down and typed up her sermons and proverbs. They recognized, without daring to speak of it, that the devotion they felt for Daisy was a kind of blasphemy. But because Daisy seemed someone who needed their protection, they could call up reserves of long-lost strength that they'd forgotten they'd ever had. Just ask any of them: they'd be happy to die finding Lenore.

As far as we know, it was actually our own Tiff who coined the name for Daisy's band of disciples: "My friend Hannah's a *Lenorian* now," she said one evening at cocktail hour. We didn't quite hear her at first, as we were all distracted by the fact that Tiff had packed her first few boxes of belongings, and the boxes sat at the front door, in plain sight, as we sipped our drinks in the dark sunroom.

So what're you going to do with my old room? Tiff had asked Doc a few days before, smiling, as if genuinely curious. Though Tiff's moving in with Ivy had been imminent for months, he'd nonetheless imagined Tiff forever indecisive, growing older nowhere else. How had she expected him to answer that question? That he'd long been wanting to take up taxidermy? That he'd be renting the room to boarders? Maybe he'd put in a few wingback chairs and a humidor and turn it into a cigar parlor, where he'd sip brandy every quiet evening alone. When he'd said, *It'll always be your room,* Tiff had seemed distraught, as if she'd hoped he'd take her cue and remain unsentimental.

Among the boxes now at the door sat her mint-green sewing machine (an old, sadly outdated one of mine, with a bobbin winder that wiggled to clumsy effect), and it seemed likely, as we stared, that it might grow legs and walk off. Even Ivy looked flustered by Tiff's leaving us. She just kept stirring her manhattan with her speared maraschino.

"Your friend is a *what?*" Doc finally asked Tiff.

"A total Lenorian," Tiff said. I'd fixed her a sloe gin and Coke, thick with cherries, but the sloe gin component was extremely minor. A matter of a drop or two or three. Probably more than that. It wasn't a regular thing. She was moving out that night, and we wanted to keep things cheerful. I offer no apologies.

"What does it mean?" Doc said.

"Her and her mom and dad go out to the Crippled Eighty every night, to sit in the field and do whatever they do," Tiff said. "Play a ukulele and sing 'Kumbaya' or whatever. You've been out there. You know what they do."

"Well, yeah, I know what they do," he said. They parked along the road and built bonfires that filled the air with the smell of mesquite. They sang hymns, and linked hands, and stood in circles, heads bowed. They shivered together in the autumn nights, sharing the hot cocoa they heated in pots plugged into their cars' cigarette lighters. They'd become less concerned with finding Lenore than with promoting her existence—they peddled faith in the girl, preaching belief in her disappearance and danger.

"But where'd you get *Lenorian?*" Doc said.

"I don't know," Tiff said. "Just kind of came up with it. Do you like it?" She smiled, perking up.

"I think I love it," he said, giving her ponytail a tug. He lifted his glass and said, "Long live the Lenorians."

We all lifted our glasses. "Long live the Lenorians," we said.

We talked about other things—how Tiff needed a new sewing machine and what we should have for supper—and the evening wore on, without supper, as none of us felt up to eating. Finally Ivy stood. She said to Tiff, "I guess we should get you . . . well, we should get you . . . you know, *home* . . . or, you know, where we live now."

It would be Tiff's first night away from Doc's

house in six years. She'd never even been to a sleepover or slumber party. She'd tried a few times, but it had made her so queasy—riding in someone else's car to someone else's house to sleep in a sleeping bag on the floor—that she'd called Doc and he'd had to go rescue her from her night of escape. In six years, we'd taken no trips; she'd had no hospitalizations. As we sat in that sunroom, Tiff's bed upstairs felt like it might fall right through the ceiling and crush us all. The headboard was still riddled with puffy little stickers—vinyl stickers of Japanese kittens with jiggly eyes—that she'd stuck there years ago. She'd outgrown the stickers, but nostalgia prevented her from peeling them off.

"Oh, I've got to get some more stuff from upstairs," Tiff said. "I'll be right back." She skipped away. We'd all been so careful to keep this transition from traumatizing the girl, and so successful at it, that she didn't seem even the tiniest bit anxious. But suddenly we felt like taking a step or two back in time, to make things a little less easy. Would it kill her to shed a few tears for our benefit?

Ivy handed Doc her glass, and it was clear how her hand shook by the sloshing of the bourbon she'd barely touched. She smiled awkwardly, then leaned into Doc, standing on her toes to kiss him on the cheek. She startled him, and he turned his head, and Ivy ended up bumping her nose hard enough to make her say, "Ouch," and to pull back, rubbing the bridge of it.

"Sorry, doll," he said, and he leaned down to kiss her cheek.

"I know it annoys you if I thank you," Ivy said, "and it's not like I'm thanking you, like you've been babysitting Tiff, I know that. I know that I can't possibly thank you. And I can't even bring myself to say—"

"Shhh," Doc said, putting a finger to her lips.

"No," she said. She slapped his hand away. "I want to say, I want to tell you . . . but I can't really say what it is that you've done for me, and for Tiff, I mean, I don't have the words, and I'm not very good at . . . well, I mean, I don't say the things I should, or that's *why* I don't say the things I should, because there's just no way to, to do it, without . . . without . . . falling apart," and she fell apart, breaking into tears, and not just a little whimpering but a storm of weeping that made her hold her head in her hands, made her sit down. "You've just made me so happy," she said. At least, that's what we thought she said—her words had devolved into sobs and hiccups.

"Do we all have to be jackasses about this?" Tiff asked, glaring at Doc, when she returned from upstairs. "What'd you do to her?"

"I raised her daughter for six years, you little snot," he said, and he thumped her head with his knuckle.

"Ouch!" she said. "Seriously! That hurt! Abuse children much?"

"That did not hurt," he said.

"It did!"

"You've got to be kidding me," Doc said. He thumped her head again with his knuckle. "You're telling me *that* hurt."

"Stop!" Tiff said, and she started pounding his arm as hard as she could, pummeling him with her fists, both of them laughing now. Doc crossed his arms and cringed, letting her gleefully beat him. But I couldn't take it anymore. Generation after generation of parents lost, of abandonment— starting with my mother's death at my birth—had left us all stunted. It wasn't funny.

"Ivy. Is crying. Her eyes out," I shouted, punctuating my melodrama with the punch of my fist in the air. I was immediately embarrassed by the silence in the room. Doc and Tiff exchanged a quick, sheepish glance, then looked down to the floor. Had I ever raised my voice to them, even once? *Dementia,* they probably thought, and perhaps rightly. I cleared my throat and spoke more calmly. I reached up to adjust the rhinestone dragonfly keeping my hair together. "I'd like for someone to attend to her, if it's not too much to ask. Can we at least *pretend* we know how to act in situations like this?"

"I'm fine, Granny, thank you," Ivy said, standing, sniffling, her voice scratchy. She cocked a hip in a housewifely fashion and threw her hands up. "I bought a cake," she announced, forcing a smile. "Would you all come over?"

"Can't," Doc said. "Granny's mad at Tiff."

"She's mad at *you*," Tiff said, punching Doc again.

I just rolled my eyes and downed the rest of my Southern Comfort. I was actually relieved they weren't taking my outburst seriously, or at least were pretending they weren't, most likely for my benefit. *Maybe they do know how to act, after all, in situations like this,* I thought. *Maybe this is exactly what people do.*

"I just have to run home and scrape the 'Happy Birthday, Katie' off it still," Ivy said. "I got it on discount. Sorry."

"You kill me, Mom," Tiff said, walking toward the door.

"Thanks for the invite," Doc said, "but I'm going to run out to the Crippled Eighty. I've got to figure out how to work the word *Lenorians* into a story and get it in this week's paper."

"Oh oh oh," Tiff said, jumpy, "are you going to need pictures?"

"Nah," he said, "I'll just use a picture I've already got."

"No, you need a new picture," Tiff said. "You need a picture of the Lenorians sitting around a fire. Praying, or something."

"Nah," he said.

"Come on, Doc," Tiff said, tugging his sleeve. "I want to go take pictures."

"This isn't the night for it, kiddo," he said. "Your mom's got cake."

"Mom's okay with it," she said. "I'll be back in plenty of time for cake. Okay, Mom?"

Ivy paused, shrugged, forced another smile. "Sure, yeah, okay, fine," she said.

"No, really," Doc said. "I don't think so. Tiff, tonight's special to your mother."

Tiff clucked her tongue and rolled her eyes. "It's been six years since I've lived with her, what's an hour or two more?"

"Tiff," Doc said, thumping her again.

"Ohhhh-kay, now," Ivy said, shooing at them both. "Go go go go go. You're not turning me into a villain over this. Just get out, do your thing, Doc will drop you off at my house after. Seriously. Not a big deal."

"You can totally come with," Tiff said.

"No," Ivy said. "I'm going home. I've got stuff to do. Katie's name isn't going to scrape *itself* off that cake."

"I love you with every beat of my heart, Mommy," Tiff said, wrapping her arms around Ivy and kissing her cheek with a comically loud *smack-smack-smack*.

"Go," Ivy said.

Doc and Tiff left, and Ivy and I stayed a bit longer in Doc's house, sitting down to one more drink. I liked to think she appreciated my sticking up for her, taking her side over Doc and Tiff's.

"They're infants," Ivy said.

"Infants," I said. We raised our glasses, toasting our babies, and we've done so ever since, every time we've had a drink together. "Infants," she always says, raising her glass, and "Infants," I say, with no explanation to anyone else.

· 27 ·

People sat cross-legged on the dry, gray ground of the field of the Crippled Eighty that night, just west of the house. Thanksgiving was still a few weeks off, and our weather had been fairly pleasant. We'd had a few cold days, and a few nights of frost, and one light snowfall of fat flakes that had melted the moment they'd touched the ground.

But the Lenorians seemed to want to rush winter, anxious to demonstrate their fortitude. They sought to create a powerful image for the national-news vans that had again returned to line the roads. Bonfires spotted the night, and singing and chanting broke through the quiet.

The lights were still on in Daisy's house. Though the indoor Lenorians had been turning all reporters away at the door, Doc was welcomed when he knocked.

"But not her," the young woman said, nodding

toward Tiff. The woman was waifish in a white muslin sundress, a bumblebee embroidered on a pocket, her hair buzzed away to just a dark stubble.

"I'd rather not leave her here on the porch," Doc said.

"She can't be on the porch either," the woman said. The woman scratched at her arms and neck as if she was wearing a wool sweater. "She needs to not be near the house."

"I have a cap," Tiff said, assuming it was the Lenore-like stark-whiteness of her hair that might shine and worry.

"I'm sorry," she said. "No little girls at all."

"Stay near one of the news trucks," Doc told Tiff. "I'll be just a few minutes."

Tiff frowned, pushing all her hair up into the stocking cap she'd wrenched onto her head.

The young woman led Doc to the kitchen table and poured him tea from a small china pot painted with a tea-party scene in pale blue: a Victorian girl in a plumed hat sipping from her cup with pinky raised. The pot and cups were very nearly the size of a child's set and unlike any Doc had seen before in the house. He looked around the kitchen. A scrambled alphabet of magnetic letters now stuck to the refrigerator door. A pink jacket hung from its hood on a pantry doorknob.

The indoor Lenorians were younger and quieter than the outdoor Lenorians, and they walked barefoot, heads bowed in cultish devotion. In the corner, on a stool, sat a shirtless young man strumming an unplugged electric guitar.

"Lenore's not a delusion," the young man said, and Doc first mistook his words for lyrics to the impromptu tune he played. Then Doc realized the man was speaking to him. "It's easier for them to try to convince everyone that she doesn't exist than it is for them to go out and find her."

"Imagine it," the young woman said, her finger making circles on top of her nearly bald head, as if she'd once been in the habit of twisting her hair. "Some asshole snags your kid," and she nodded toward the window, toward Tiff, presumably, "and when you call the cops, they tell you your kid wasn't real enough. How effed up is that?" When she saw Daisy enter the doorway, she stepped forward quickly to pull out a chair. Daisy wore the daisy-print dress.

"Thanks for letting them let me in," Doc said.

Daisy sat down and shrugged. "It's your story now too," she said. She lifted the lid of the teapot and looked inside.

"Plum spice," the young woman said. "You want some?"

Daisy shook her head.

"A gift?" Doc said. "That tea set?"

"I don't know," Daisy said. "The children bring things in, they take things out." Doc looked at the young woman again; now that Daisy had labeled her a child, he noticed she seemed older than he'd first suspected—crow's feet cracked out from her eyes, and her teeth had a nicotine tint.

"How long have they all . . ." Doc started, but Daisy shook her head and brought her finger to her lips for a shushing.

"I have something very specific to tell you," Daisy said. "I won't take questions."

"Okay," Doc said.

"You're not going to write it down?" she said.

Doc took a digital recorder from his pocket and set it on the table before him. Daisy reached across to slide it closer to her. "Lenore won't be the last missing little girl they say never existed," she said. She leaned over to speak into the recorder, her arms crossed at her chest. "Ever notice how they don't put missing kids' pictures on milk cartons anymore? Got to be a reason for it, don't you think? And it's not because nobody's kids are gone. A child goes missing every forty seconds." She looked up at the young woman. "How long have we been talking here, Cassie?"

The young woman glanced at her wrist, but she wore no watch. "I'd say a good forty seconds," she said, though it had seemed to Doc that minutes had passed.

"So one whole child's been kidnapped while we sit here talking about Lenore, a girl who should've been found more than ten weeks ago," Daisy said. "Ten weeks is 6,048,000 seconds. Divide that by forty. That's 151,200 missing kids. You don't have to be a math whiz to understand the implications of turning our back on Lenore. She's more than just one little girl now. She's tens of thousands of little girls." Daisy pushed the recorder back across the table.

"Daisy," Doc said, "how many people are in—"

She interrupted him again by standing from the table, shaking her head. "Go home and go to bed," she said.

Doc stood and bumped his head on a little white bamboo birdcage that housed the light bulb above the table. Before, the bulb had been covered by a dusty globe; Doc remembered the shadows of the husks of dead bugs collecting at the bottom of it. As he lifted his hand to stop the cage from rocking, Daisy left the room.

Cassie took Doc by the arm and led him toward the front door. "You'd better go find your little girl," she said. "I'm a little worried about her."

Doc became worried too when he stepped into the yard and saw no sign of Tiff. And his worry failed to ease even after he found her. "Coo-coo," Tiff called down from the upper branches of a fir next to the house. "Coo-coo."

Before he was able to even finish his fateful sentence—"What are you trying to do, break your neck?"—Tiff fell, slowing her descent by grabbing at the branches she passed, skinning herself. She lay in the needles as Doc reached her, staring up at her camera dangling above them caught by its strap.

"Are you okay?" Doc asked, desperate to see Tiff nod her head. She did nod, her finger stuck in her mouth.

"I think I nearly bit my tongue out of my head, though," she said. "My tongue look okay to you?" She opened her mouth, and Doc aimed the beam of his penlight inside. He squinted.

"It looks fine," he said, "but tongues are weird."

"Climb up and get my camera," she said. "I got some shots of a few Lenorians in an upstairs room playing cards."

"You don't say," Doc said. He was furious, but you never could tell with Doc. When peeved, he grew aloof, as if he couldn't be bothered with being annoyed by someone so foolish. "Unless it's dogs playing poker, I don't know if the juice was worth the squeeze on this one, punk."

"You really shouldn't be mad at me," she said. She lay back on the ground, her hand at her forehead. "I'm still rattled."

"Get up," he said. "We're getting in the car. This is your mother's night." He nudged her shoulder with his foot.

"Yeah, you've said that lots already. This is my first night in my mom's house. It's important. I get it."

"Don't you want to go there tonight?" he said.

"No, I do," she said. Doc sat on the ground next

to her. Something rustled in the ditch, a rabbit most likely, crackling through the dried weeds. "Her feelings are going to get hurt when I peel all those glow-in-the-dark stars off the ceiling. But I'm going to have to get used to hurting her feelings. Unless I pretend I'm six for the rest of my life, her feelings are going to get hurt. It's exhausting."

"If I knew you were going to climb trees and fall out of them, I never would've let you come along," Doc said. "I shouldn't have left you out here by yourself. I know you're not six years old, but you're not as old as you think you are."

"You have no idea how old I am," she said.

He nudged her shoulder again. "Get up," he said. "Let's get out of here. I'm going to be up all night writing about your stupid Lenorians."

"You still have to climb up and get my camera," she said. She rolled onto her side, away from Doc, and curled up, fetal. "I'm glad we were able to have this little talk," she said, and though Doc suspected, from the way she sighed, that she meant to be sarcastic, he couldn't help but hear a twitch of sincerity in her voice.

"If you're being mouthy to me," Doc said, "I don't appreciate it, frankly. Is this how you are, now that you're a teenager? If it is, you're not aging well."

"Are you scolding me?" Tiff asked, propping herself up on her elbow. "It sounds like you're scolding me."

"No," he said.

He stepped into the tree and up a few branches, but when he reached for the camera, he stopped. His fingers brushed across paper. In a crook of the tree, Doc discovered a ragged, short plank of wood. Back on the ground, he shone his light on the plank—it had been part of a thin, makeshift wall papered with a print of tiny red roses. Curving around and among the roses was a minuscule, mostly illegible scrawl. Doc could read only random words across the plank—*friend, heart, mouse, blue, thistle, sleep.*

"You gotta be kiddin' me," Tiff said when Doc showed her the plank. "That's a girl's hand-writing." Tiff's finger traced the path of the sentences among the roses, and she recalled, once again, how Doc had often promised to build her a playhouse in the backyard, with a little stove that baked cakes with a light bulb. *Sleeping baby,* she read. Or maybe it said, *creeping early.* Or *leaping fatly.* Or *slugging eels, slurping brain, keeping flap.*

There were many other words written on the plank as well, and as Tiff and Doc attempted to read them aloud, the letters seemed to dissolve into hieroglyphics, the child-like scribble jumbling into knots.

"This could've come from anywhere," Doc said. "That tornado last spring had sticky fingers. It'd lift something from one farm and drop it

124

smack-dab in some wacky place." It had indeed been a fickle breeze. In the aftermath back in June, we'd taken a drive along the country roads, surveying the wreckage. A billboard advertising itself *(This Space Available)* had been lifted from its posts and cradled in sagging power lines. The north wall of Eleanor Allen's house had been peeled away, and we'd seen that her piano had been pushed from the parlor into the kitchen. Eleanor had told us later that her book of gospel songs had nonetheless remained open to the same hymn.

"Who are you calling?" Tiff asked Doc.

"The sheriff," he said, flipping open his cell phone. At that, Tiff grabbed the plank from the ground and ran toward the back of the house. Doc could've caught up with her; he could've stopped her, and he knew he should've. But he was already growing accustomed to what seemed to be his new role: the permissive parent. It was cruel to do that to Ivy, he knew. But if she wanted motherhood, she could have it. He, meanwhile, would let Tiff fall from trees.

Tiff let herself in the back screen door and walked up to the kitchen table, the plank held out before her like a shiv, where Daisy sat with a deck of cards. Tiff might have looked suspect, had anyone bothered to notice her. Though three Lenorians hovered, Daisy played solitaire. She gazed down at the splay of cards, caught in a deep concentration, her thumb inching the top card back and forth across the stack in her hand.

"It's all right," Doc told them all as he entered the kitchen, before there was even a hint of alarm. But once the Lenorians caught sight of Tiff, her angel-white hair a fright wig of nettles and static, the plank held before her like a water-witching stick, they came to life, poised to wrestle the girl away from Daisy's sight. "It's okay, Daisy," Doc said. "She's mine. She's with me."

"Look at this," Tiff told Daisy.

Daisy, unbothered, seemed to be seeing it and not seeing it at the same time. Her thumb still worked at that top card. She then put down the deck. She reached up and walked her fingers across the plank lightly, spider-like.

"Tell me what it is," Tiff said.

Daisy shrugged.

"She doesn't know," the buzz-headed Lenorian said, pushing the plank away from Daisy.

"Look at the handwriting," Tiff said, pushing it back toward Daisy. "Are you seeing the handwriting? Do you recognize it?"

Daisy looked past the plank at Tiff. "Does it say where Lenore is?"

"Nooooo," Tiff said slowly, as if speaking to a child. "It doesn't say anything that makes sense. But it was in a tree near the house."

"You need to leave," said the Lenorian with the guitar, but he made no movement toward Tiff.

"What's your name?" Daisy asked, and Tiff told her. *"Tiff?"* Daisy said.

"Tiff," Tiff said. "Short for Tiffany."

Daisy nodded, tilted her head to the side. "Tiffany," she said, "if it doesn't tell me where to go to get Lenore, then I don't see much reason to bother reading it." Daisy's spirits seemed suddenly to lift. She straightened up in her chair and held her folded hands beneath her breasts in a matriarchal pose of utmost serenity. "Every day but Sunday the mailman brings to this house a bagful of letters; some of them have nothing but 'The Crippled Eighty' written on the envelope, but they all find their way here to me. All that sympathy, all that advice. People who've lost their own children, writing to offer condolence. Miles and miles of letters that lead me nowhere. Newspaper article after newspaper article." She glanced toward Doc, then back to Tiff. "Thousands of words. Why does anyone read any of it if it doesn't change anything? If everything's still the same when you get to the end, then haven't you given up part of your life to the person with all the words? This stranger just telling stories to be telling them?"

"Yeah, okay," Tiff said. "Yeah, I understand. But you don't have to *read* anything. Just look at the writing. If you recognize it, then maybe that will actually *help* them get to Lenore."

"How?" Daisy said. "Because if I tell you that

Lenore wrote those words, then maybe that's proof that she exists? Because we still don't believe in her, do we? But even if that is Lenore's writing, it doesn't prove that she exists, Tiffany. I don't know if she exists. She could've been killed minutes after she was taken from me, or hours, or weeks. He could've killed her while I sit here talking, or he could kill her tomorrow. I'm no longer an authority on Lenore's existence. As a matter of fact, I hope to God that everyone who says I'm crazy is right. I hope Lenore has always been a figment of my imagination. Don't you?"

· 28 ·

Sitting in Doc's car, parked in front of Ivy's house, the motor running, Tiff held the plank on her lap, tracing her finger along the twist of the sentences, describing for Doc her theories. The tornado took Lenore, Tiff explained, sweeping the girl into its spin, stealing her breath and leaving her deflated and tangled in a fence. "And Daisy just wanted to block it all out," Tiff said. "She destroyed everything of Lenore's then—took a hatchet to her playhouse, burned her clothes. And now she doesn't remember Lenore blowing away at all. She convinced herself that Lenore is still alive somewhere."

"Far-fetched," Doc said.

Tiff shrugged. "We'll see," she said. She looked

to the pink house and the bright glow of its porch light. Ivy sat by the front picture window, pretending to be so engrossed in a book that she didn't notice Doc's car out front. "She waited up," Tiff said.

"Of course she did," Doc said.

"I do feel sorry for her," Tiff said.

"Why?" Doc said.

Tiff shrugged again. "Because I'm not really a little girl anymore, I guess," she said. "I think she'd like it better if I was the same little girl she left."

Doc tried to think of something supportive to say but could come up with nothing. Defending Ivy took a level of imagination he didn't have at that late hour. He pushed in the cigarette lighter, though it hadn't worked in years. He fiddled with the volume on the radio. "Ivy loves you," he finally said.

Tiff held her hands to her face to cry. Throughout her childhood, Doc had cradled Tiff in his arms many times as she'd wept. He'd rocked her; he'd kissed the top of her head. But he had no idea what to do with a crying thirteen-year-old. One wrong move and he'd make things ten times worse, he feared. He reached over to pat her shoulder. It didn't seem enough, so he squeezed her shoulder too.

"I'm okay," she said. "I guess I'm just a little homesick already."

Doc didn't tell her that he was pleased to hear it, but he did smile one of those sympathetic smiles that look like a flinch—his face squeezed into a little grimace, and he nodded.

"We're always just down the street," Doc told her.

"For now," Tiff said. "I'm afraid Great-Granny's going to die someday soon."

"Your great-granny's going to outlive us all," he said. "She's already outlived two husbands. A son. A daughter-in-law. She's clearly cursed. You should be afraid to be around her." Tiff sniffled out a laugh, probably just to be polite. "And the way you went storming into Daisy's with that plank, you're lucky to be alive. Those Lenorians might be packing heat."

"I thought Daisy would be excited to see it," she said. "But she wouldn't even look at it."

"We shouldn't have taken it from the tree," Doc said. "We've kind of disturbed evidence."

Tiff nodded, then hugged the plank to her chest. "I'm going to take some pictures of it and e-mail them to you," she said.

"Wait till morning," he said. "You need to eat some of that cake your mom bought for you."

"No need to worry about us, Uncle Doc," Tiff said. She patted his hand and then opened the car door. Doc wasn't sure what *us* she meant. Him and her? Her and Ivy? Who didn't she think he should worry about?

· 29 ·

In the morning, a few hours into daylight, we all joined the sheriff and his deputies in the pasture, where he'd found more planks of handwriting. In the dry creek bed at a dip in the pasture were the charred remnants of some of the farm's branches and wrecked structures from the previous spring's tornado. Back then, the deep, dark nights across the countryside had been spotted with firelight, the farmers burning away the ruins of their houses and barns.

Not everything had burned away in Daisy's effort. Though she'd lost mostly trees in the storm, among the branches in the pile in the creek bed were parts of small buildings—half a door, shingles, a bench, the rungs of a ladder. And when a deputy pushed through the refuse with a garden hoe, he unearthed more of the marked-up planks, the wallpaper ashen and curling but no less revelatory.

The house is on fire, one line of graffiti seemed to read before the words untangled before our eyes and snaked away into other shapes. *The winter is alive,* it said next. For weeks afterward, every bit of writing I passed became words they weren't—*Fines Double* on a highway sign was *Bones Fragile* for a brief, murky moment. *No vacancy* in red neon promised *Novocain.*

131

We pinned many hopes on the expertise of Astrid Jacobs, a handwriting analyst who worked for the state. Technically, she kept reminding us, she was a *forensic document examiner*—hers was a scientific endeavor, to solve crimes and settle disputes, involving an intimate understanding of ink and paper, of the paint of graffiti on concrete; she'd even once determined the whereabouts of a kidnapper by studying the loops and hangs of the lettering of frosting on a cake. Handwriting analysis, a carnival act called *graphology,* was empty razzle-dazzle, she said, with all it claimed to reveal about personality and tendencies. It was of the school of palmistry and tarot, whereas her work had effectively put men away for life.

Astrid was nearly my age, and her vision was still crystal-clear, her hand steady. She could identify someone by the slant of a letter in a signature, could find fraud in the lazy smear of an erasure in a ledger book. In 1966, she'd once cracked a case in six seconds just by scratching her thumbnail against a dot of Wite-Out, revealing a telltale decimal point. But her confidence, a key element of discovery, had weakened. Crimes now were solved by computer experts tracing digital paths or summoning up echoes of old conversations—deleted chat logs and e-mails in the recesses of a computer's memory. Communication had become a bowl of alphabet soup, with the illiterate shorthand of text messages and the millions of fonts at everyone's fingertips. Where in all of that was the mark of the primitive individual?

What can you tell us? we asked, holding forth the plank of wood.

"Inconclusive," Astrid said. She said the scribbles could be those of a young girl. Or not. She said they could be Daisy's effort to simulate a child's writing. Or not. "It could be something," she said, "or it could be nothing."

But the images of the plank, the words and half sentences, ran in newspapers and on websites around the world, resulting in new lines of scrutiny—the words became pieces of puzzles and sources of theories. One man, after deciphering the words and applying numbers based on the letters' places in the alphabet, devised a code that revealed Lenore's approximate whereabouts *(a blue rowboat in a Southern river at a crumbling dock in a weedy delta)*, while another man interpreted the language as poetic prophesy predicting Lenore's own abduction. And a handwriting analyst—a practitioner of the mumbo-jumbo Astrid ridiculed—gauged Lenore's personality by studying the direction of her cursive. Lenore was impulsive yet cautious; tough yet delicate.

All the new speculation, and the reporters' pursuit of Daisy to speculate on that speculation, sent Daisy into a new period of solitude. One day, on what became known as Blue Sunday among the Lenorians, Daisy threw them all from her home. She grabbed them by their arms and shoved them toward the door. She yanked at their collars and slapped at their backs. The Lenorians, particularly the young ones, the runaways driven to the Crippled Eighty to escape addiction and cruelty, had no idea where to go.

Part

· 30 ·

O n Thanksgiving morning, Tiff appeared to levitate above a makeshift stage in the dining hall of the nursing home. She wore silver slippers, pajama bottoms patterned with pink elephants, and a fake-fur shrug over an old T-shirt. Yellow feathers were clipped in her hair. She lay back on a thin board above two trick folding chairs.

Doc and Tiff had performed magic at the Willow House every Thanksgiving morning for the last four years—their showstopper was a dollar bill bursting into flame to light Tiff's exploding cigar. Usually I stayed home to cook, but this year Ivy had insisted on hosting Thanksgiving in her home. She'd spent the week sprinkling glitter on pinecones for decoration and experimenting with mincemeat-pie recipes culled from old cookbooks.

So Tiff had dragged me to the Willow House, where I refused to remove my coat. I kept my purse in my lap. Not only were these people close to my age, some slightly older, some slightly younger, but I'd known many of them for years. Some had been prominent members of the community—there was a park in our town named after one of the men, and one of the women had owned a café on one corner of the town square for fifty years. I'd written the obituaries of some of them already and filed them in a folder marked *Impending Doom*.

It's not what you're thinking. I'm actually opposed to what I call the itchy-trigger-finger method of obit writing—before a celebrity has even choked out his famous last words, the writers of the world thrill to be the first to bear bad news, so they keep obits of the notable written and at the ready. But, in all modesty, I've written obits of the local elderly only because they've asked me to. I've been in the business for so long, since my girlhood, that I've created portraits of these people's grandparents, their parents, even some of their children. I'm as much a part of the traditions of death as a gilded lily.

Doc ran a large silver hoop over Tiff to demonstrate that there were no hidden wires. People kindly applauded, but no one seemed amazed. Doc released Tiff from her hovering, lowering her to the chairs. She extracted herself from the illusion, stepped to the front of the stage, and curtsied. "Thank you, thank you, ladies and gents," Doc said, pulling a bouquet of ugly flowers from his top hat.

"Essie?" said someone to my left. There stood an old, old woman, still quite lovely, with thick gray hair and wet blue eyes. She wore a silky white gown, and she put her hand on my shoulder. Was she the angel of my own impending doom?

To die while visiting a nursing home, how perfect, I thought, but there were any number of perfect deaths for a writer of obituaries. Any end would be fitting. To simply slip away some night in my sleep would seem almost ironic.

"Bernice," she said, reminding me. Of course. My dear Bernice, who had, since our youth, always been the prettier of the two of us. Her life had been a dream, every minute of it unmarked by tragedy, so, naturally, we'd drifted apart years before. With my own life having been so slipshod, I must've been a nagging reminder that, in a heartbeat, everything good could be lost.

I took Bernice's hand, just for a friendly squeeze, but she held on to mine, so we stayed that way, holding hands, as we spoke. "I thought you'd moved in with your kids," I said.

"I did," she said, "but I just kept falling, falling, falling. Breaking things, breaking myself. I'm just skin and bones anymore. And not good skin and not good bones."

It did feel as if, even with my weakling's grip, I could shatter the bones in her hand with little effort, and maybe that was what made me feel so overcome with affection for her just then. I wanted to take her home with me, where we could live our last days as eccentric relics, doddering and afflicted, our once-a-week curl-and-sets falling apart lock by lock together. We could endlessly reminisce, live in the past to an unhealthy degree, then politely kill each other some winter night before bedtime, stirring poison into our cups of whiskey-spiked chamomile tea, wearing party hats. Then, nervous about our double homicide, we could lie in bed together, holding hands again, frightened and waiting, still wondering, after all these years, if we even believed in our own souls.

Bernice pulled her hand away. "Well, you take care, Essie," she said with what I interpreted as a privileged tone of dismissal, and just like that, my fantasy of our last-ditch life together dissolved. Bernice shuffled off, content with how things had gone for her. She had no need for a pact of any kind.

And neither did I, damn it. I would *not* be one of those people, weepy and spiteful, who they had to drag, kicking and screaming, to her hole in the ground. It was someone else's turn to have a long life of writing obituaries. I did indeed, I was certain, have it in me to bow out gracefully. I vowed right then to retire, to leave them all wanting more. I'd write my last obituary—for Bernice—and I'd tuck it into my file of impending doom.

· 31 ·

At Ivy's, Doc and Tiff set the table for the Thanksgiving dinner they dreaded—Ivy had prepared a menu based on a mid-nineteenth-century cookbook, and from the gamy smell of things, they didn't know what to expect. *Skinned porcupine?* Doc had whispered to Tiff. *Pickled oysters?* Tiff had whispered back.

Doc stood at Ivy's china cabinet, running his finger along the rim of a wineglass. "All these wineglasses have chips in them," he said. Ivy had bought the glasses, and the cabinet, and the whole dining room set, just days before at a garage sale. A week ago the dining room had had nothing in it but a folding chair and a card table with Tiff's sewing machine. Now there was a long table that seated eight, eight creaky, scuffed-up chairs, the cabinet full of someone else's best china, and a reproduction of a painting, in a gold-painted frame, of an old man praying over a loaf of bread.

"Those glasses are chipped?" Ivy said. She wiped her hands on her apron as she walked in from the kitchen. "I thought I had checked them over good."

"I'll just call Granny and have her bring some of hers over," Doc said.

"Granny's already here," I said, stepping in, still in my fur coat, my purse on my arm, leaning on the umbrella I often used as a cane. "But I'm on my way out already. I'm not staying."

Too dramatic, I confess, but I also confess that it felt satisfying to silence the room. I'd been dramatic before, certainly, sending everyone scurrying for remedies. A banal palpitation you've known since youth can seem, in old age, morbidly foreshadowing. I've had a very occasional nervous twitching in my eyelid, for example, since grade school, which first reared up during a math test—now I can manage to convince myself that that slight flutter has never been harmless at all, but rather a sign that I'm about to go blind.

"I want to visit my sister," I said. "Her nursing home is about an hour's drive each way, and I don't want to be driving in the dark, and it gets dark so early."

"She won't know you, Essie," Tiff said, tilting her head with concern.

"Sometimes she knows me," I said. "No one else is going to visit her today."

"We should never have taken you to the Willow House," Doc said. "It's made you morose."

"We'll drive you," Tiff said.

"No, absolutely not," I said. "Your mother's been cooking."

"I've been cooking for three days," Ivy said, pressing her thumb against the chip in the wineglass. Her dinner was derived from the Thanksgiving depicted in *The Plumes and the*

Feathers, one of Myrtle Kingsley Fitch's first novels—some bit of hard-biscuit prose about the mail-order German bride of a crotchety homesteader and the serenity she finds in her dying turnip patch—originally published in serial form in an early-twentieth-century women's magazine.

Ivy's interest in Myrtle Kingsley Fitch had risen from a harmless, useless literature course she'd once taken at the university, for self-improvement. She had regularly left Tiff with Doc to drive the three hours to campus on Tuesday nights, but by midterm, she hadn't been coming home until Thursdays; by November, she hadn't been coming home at all. By finals week, she'd booked her flight to Paris, where she would serve for the spring semester as a research assistant for her lit professor, a noted Myrtle Kingsley Fitch scholar. Myrtle Kingsley Fitch had left Nebraska for Paris in the 1920s, and she'd lived there, with a lesbian chef, until she'd died. In Paris were original documents in private collections and college libraries—handwritten love letters to and fro, royalty statements, notes penciled into the margins of books, an incomplete, unpublished erotic novel written under the nom de plume *Mme. Marie Moth-Scryff.* When the professor's sabbatical had expired that August, he'd returned to Nebraska and his faculty wife, and Ivy had stayed in Paris to write him long, poetic letters promising an ugly suicide while she'd clerked in a boutique on the Champs-Élysées, selling perfumey French-milled soap to tourists. For years, Ivy had written those urgent suicide notes.

I've been cooking for three days, she had the nerve to tell me when I told her I was going to visit my lonely, dying, twisted sister on Thanksgiving. *Three days is absolutely nothing,* I wanted to answer. Then I wanted to say, *No, it's worse than nothing. It's something, then it's gone in a blink.*

But instead I said, "I promise to be back before everything's completely ruined." I turned and left before Doc even thought to offer me his car to drive.

I would return in one piece, but only just barely, just after dark. But before that, while I sat shaken on the roadside in my pickup, my heart pumping at a troubling beat, petting the fur of my coat for ease, my family waited for me. They all sat at the ornate table, complete with tarnished silver napkin rings, not eating a bite as Ivy's complicated sauces clotted in their pans in the kitchen and the wind outside picked up. The wind chimes rattled like they were being rolled down a hill. Doc and Ivy drank from the wineglasses, careful to avoid the chips in the rims.

"Fold your hands together," Tiff said, her sketchbook in her lap.

"You're drawing *me?*" Doc said.

"No, I'm doing a self-portrait," she said. "But I need to see how the fingers go."

So Doc posed without another word, slouching like Tiff slouched. He was always telling her to sit up straight.

· *32* ·

M y sister always used to fall asleep in the car. One time, when we were young women, and neither of our boyfriends had cars, I'd driven us all toward a far-off lake. Lydia had slept in the backseat in her swimsuit, a beach towel across her knees, and she'd wakened just long enough to say, "The last time I drove, remember, Essie? I fell asleep at the wheel. I woke up and thought we were driving through a forest of spindly trees, but it was a cornfield, and we survived." That was all she'd said before dozing off again.

"Do you remember that, Lydia?" I asked her as I sat next to her in the TV room of the nursing home. Like the Willow House, the building was noisy with the squawking of television after television in room after room. I often felt that my house was too quiet, even with music on, but if I lived in a place like this, I would scream for complete silence. I'd beg for the quiet of the grave.

Lydia took a deep breath and rocked in her wheelchair. "I'll tell you a little about what I know, then I'll tell you a little about what I don't know," she said, but then she didn't say anything else.

"It's a holiday, Lydie," I said. "I bet that's something that you know. Your Thanksgiving dinners, you remember those, I know you do, you can't *not* remember those. You were the best cook anywhere in the world. I never could've predicted how much I'd miss your cooking. It's heartbreaking how much I miss it. Your fried chicken! How'd you get it that way?" I playfully, lightly slapped her wrist.

"Follow the recipe," she said.

"I've tried, Lydie," I said.

"No, you're afraid to use enough shortening," she said.

"Ivy made something terrible today, I just know it," I said. "The house smelled like fish. I wanted to blow my brains out. Is this the way it's going to be? From now on? If I have any Thanksgivings left?"

"Ivy is your sister?"

"No, Lydie, *you're* my sister."

"My sister died," she said, dismissive, returning her gaze to an episode of an old cop show, everyone in bell-bottoms.

"I know you don't mean that," I said. I tugged at a loose thread in the seam of the sleeve of her housecoat. I twisted it around my finger and pulled at it more. "Your hair looks pretty," I said. "You must've got it done."

"I'd love to have her fried chicken again," she said, sighing. She helped me tug the thread from the seam. "Wouldn't you? But my sister died, and she made it the best. It was something terrible, though. Smelled like fish. She used too much shortening."

A man who I could've sworn was the late Edward Mack, an area farmer, shuffled by in flannel pajamas, a bandage wrapped tight around his head. Not only had he died, I was certain, but I'd written his obituary. He'd perished rather memorably, ignobly, a few months before, in a freak accident involving an augur and a loose shoelace. Had I somehow jumped to conclusions? Maybe I was the senile one. Maybe I lived here, always in my fur coat, my purse always on my arm, poised for home.

"You're getting everything confused," I said. "*You* were the cook. You weren't just good, you were a genius. You could've cooked for kings, Lydia."

"It's so very, very slight, but you really notice it," she said. "Golden delicious. The apples in your stuffing. It makes all the difference. Anything other than golden delicious in there, and you end up with something you don't want." She put her hand on my wrist. "I'd fix you something before you go, but I always fall asleep in the kitchen."

"No," I said, "you always fall asleep in the car, not in the kitchen."

"Well," she said, sighing again, returning her gaze to the TV. "I guess you'd be the only one who'd know."

It was getting dark even earlier than I'd expected it to. "I need to get home, love," I said. "I promised the kids."

"The kids," she said, sneering. "When you're a kid, they tell you, *Better enjoy it now*."

"And we did, Lydia," I said. "We really did. We had a hell of a time." I stood, kissed her cheek, and wished her a good night.

On the way home, driving slowly on the interstate, I thought it such a shame that our culture had not devised a way to defang old age. A sophisticated civilization wouldn't ridicule senility, it would elevate it, worship it, wouldn't it? We would train ourselves to see poetry in the nonsense of dementia, to actually look forward to becoming so untethered from the world. We'd make a ceremony of casting off our material goods and confining ourselves to a single room, leaving all our old, abandoned space to someone new, someone young, so that we could die alone, indifferent to our own decay and lost beauty.

In my midnight letter to Muscatine, I would write, *If I told you I was driven off the road by a truck just then, as I was distracted by my thoughts of nearing death, would you even believe me, especially considering the tidily ironic conversation I'd just had with my sister about her sleeping in cars? Would you believe, no less, that my typewriter, my tool in chiming the death knell, sat next to me on the seat of my pickup?* I'd retrieved the typewriter just the day before from the jeweler on the town square who always repaired it for me—its carriage return had gone glitchy—and I'd not yet returned it to my desk. There'd been no recent deaths in the county to report. As my pickup left the pavement and bounced across the hard dirt, the typewriter's keys clacked frantically, and its bell rang, as if speeding to meet a deadline.

So my instinct, to keep you believing me, Mr. Muscatine, is to twist the truth. That truck did not come into my lane, and I didn't drive off the road to avoid it. I didn't sit there afterward, shivering with fear, as the truck roared and rumbled on, oblivious to some frail old lady's daily brush with mortality.

To be honest, I couldn't tell the truth even if I wanted to. My eyesight is not good after dark, and I was quite tired and emotional. That truck may not have come into my lane at all. It seemed to be inching over, growing louder, repelling my car with a reverse magnetism, but maybe my morbid imagination invested the truck with malevolent intent. Maybe I was just thinking of Lydia asleep at the wheel.

I turned off the pickup and listened to the wind whistling through a crack in the window. I huddled into my fur. Tiff had loved my coat when she'd been small, but now she despised it.

"I can't believe you keep wearing it," she'd told me a few days before.

"You used to call it *Trudy*," I told her. "You would beg me to put Trudy on so that you could fall asleep in my arms petting it."

Someone stood at the window of my pickup, tapping the glass, a young man and woman in stocking caps and face piercings. "Please go away," I said. I guess they reminded me of the meth addicts I'd written about last winter, a newlywed couple who'd frozen to death in the subzero night. "Please," I said. "I have no money. Please, I beg you, go away."

"No, no," the woman said, pressing her hand flat against the glass. She smiled. "No, ma'am. We just stopped to make sure you're okay. Are you all right?" I looked over to their car stopped on the shoulder. They'd turned on their emergency flashers. There was a child, a toddler, sleeping in a car seat in the back.

"We can make a call for you," the man said, holding up his cell phone. "We can call anyone you want us to."

"How terrible of me," I said, embarrassed. "I'm

sorry. I'm so sorry. Ignore me, I'm a crazy woman. *You* aren't safe from *me*."

"Don't apologize," the girl said through the glass. She winked. "He's pretty scary, particularly with that long, curly hair like a girl."

I put my hand against the glass, where her hand was. "I'm just fine, sweetheart," I said. "I'm very good. But could you tell me what you saw? Did that truck come into my lane?"

"We didn't see what happened," she said. "We just saw your pickup sitting here and wanted to make sure everything was okay."

"Why don't you go ahead and start your car and drive back onto the highway?" the man said. "We'll follow you."

"You're too kind," I said. "Let me give you something. I lied before, I have money. I want to give you something to thank you for stopping."

The woman pulled her hand from the glass and waved the offer away. "Absolutely not," she said. "You have a happy Thanksgiving," she said.

I really wish they wouldn't stop for people, I thought, driving back onto the pavement. I worried about them, so vulnerable, with that child. I looked in my rearview mirror at their headlights. I could've been a trap. I could've been bait for something sinister. They'd had no way of knowing. They eventually passed me, the man waving, the woman pressing her hand against the glass of her window. I put my hand against my window too.

· 33 ·

For her cell phone's ringtone, Tiff was using the screams of a woman being knifed in an Italian horror movie. In the middle of the night of Thanksgiving Day, Tiff's friend Nat, knowing of the chronic insomnia that had plagued Tiff since the age of seven, tried calling Tiff repeatedly, setting off the screams again and again. But Tiff had forgotten her phone in the living room and was upstairs in her bed, watching, with earphones deafening her to the rest of the world, another Italian horror movie on her laptop. The screams woke Ivy, and though she knew they were unlikely real, they were nonetheless unsettling.

Ivy went downstairs in her ex-lover's pajamas. She'd been wearing Prof. Chester's flannel pajamas, pajamas she'd bought him for Christmas in Paris, for so many years that they'd faded from a sky blue to a near-white. In an ugly scene, as he'd packed to leave her five years before, she had unpacked everything he'd put in the suitcase.

"Stop being an infant," he said. Prof. Chester grabbed her by the arm, lifted her away from his clothes, and shoved her against the wall, where she tumbled and fell against an end table, rapping her funny bone hard and breaking a lamp. Ivy sat there, sobbing.

"Where am I supposed to go?" she cried. They'd been subleasing the apartment from another professor, also on sabbatical. He would be returning in a week.

"Go home to your family," he told her. He needed nothing at all from her—not forgiveness, not respect. *She's been my wife for twenty-five years,* he'd told Ivy when he'd announced he was going back to Mrs. Chester. *That's important to me.* "You have a child," he told Ivy. "You know, that was one of the things that first attracted me to you. A young single mother, taking a night class, improving her life. It was touching. When I suggested you coming to France with me, quite frankly, I was surprised that you said you would. And kind of disappointed, in a way. So things, for us, started falling apart from the very beginning. You weren't who I thought you were if it was so easy for you to leave your little girl."

The screams of the phone had stopped by the time Ivy reached the kitchen at the bottom of the stairs. She cocked her head, perked her ears, listening to the house. Her watch, left on the kitchen counter, *tick-tock*ed louder than she realized it ever did when it was on her wrist. A rack rattled in the fridge as the motor ran, causing wine bottles to jingle. She reached in to stop the jingling, then decided to empty the almost-empty bottle of chardonnay. Earlier she'd thrown away the chipped wineglasses, but now she pulled one from the trash, rinsed it off, and poured herself the last glass of wine.

Ivy took a needle and thread from a kitchen drawer to repair a button of the pajamas. She'd also kept two of her professor's shirts and a necktie, all of which she still wore. Perverse, she realized, but Prof. Chester, villain though he was, was the great lost love of her life. She didn't want it to be that way—it wasn't a romantic notion she'd concocted. It just was. She'd contemplated, now that she was back from France, signing up for another of his courses. She fantasized sitting in the first row on the first day of class, stunning in a long white winter coat, doused in the French perfume he used to buy her. *Prof. Chester,* she'd say, raising her hand, *why, in your scholarship, do you so aggressively refute the lesbian interpretations of Myrtle Kingsley Fitch's* The Ladies of the Katydids? *Is it because of Mrs. Chester's history of lesbian affairs throughout your marriage, including one with one of your colleagues at this very university? Is it because of your own feelings of inadequacy in keeping your wife satisfied that you fear careful analysis of gender roles?*

After Prof. Chester had left her in Paris, returning to his wife, Ivy had answered an ad in the newspaper—a woman seeking a roommate. So Ivy kept her money in savings and lived for five years in a small bedroom, afraid to return to

Nebraska for the very reason she'd left in the first place—she was a terrible mother for Tiffany. She worried she'd be even worse if she returned so heartbroken. She had thought Prof. Chester would take care of her forever. He would've taken them in, and he would've helped her provide for her daughter. She'd been so enraptured by that portrait of the rest of her life that her life was not easily reimagined. She stayed in France because she thought that might win Prof. Chester back. Within a year, as a woman of Paris, he'd want her again, she reasoned.

Ivy heard the horror-movie screaming again and followed it to the living room, where the cell phone sat on a sofa cushion. She answered it.

"Is Tiff there?" the girl on the phone said.

"Of course not," Ivy said. "She's in bed." She then said, "Do you realize what time it is?" only because it was something that every parent eventually said.

"Oh, I'm sorry," the girl said. "This is Tiff's friend Nat. Usually she's up. Because of her insomnia."

"Tiff doesn't have insomnia," Ivy said.

"Oh," Nat said. "Okay. But she does, kind of. She's had it since she was little. We talk in the middle of the night all the time. I have insomnia too, ever since my parents split up."

"I can't imagine," Ivy said.

"Well, I'm very sorry I bothered you," Nat said.

"I'll just text her. She can read it in the morning, I guess, but she'll really, really, really want to know about it."

"Happy Thanksgiving, Nat," Ivy said. Ivy closed the phone and sat on the sofa in the dark, finishing her wine. In a few minutes, the phone chimed and lit up with its text message. Ivy flipped open the phone and dialed, with one thumb, Prof. Chester's house. *Stop calling here,* Mrs. Chester had told Ivy once, years before, but it had sounded less like a demand than a plea. *He won't talk to you. And I won't let him change our number because we've had the same number for our whole marriage. We are not changing this number.*

The phone rang, but Ivy hung up. Leaving an unfamiliar phone number on their caller ID, in the middle of the night: it satisfied Ivy.

Ivy went back upstairs and opened Tiff's door. Tiff looked startled and pulled the plugs from her ears and slapped shut her laptop. "I couldn't sleep," Tiff said.

"Apparently you never sleep," Ivy said. "Nat says you're an insomniac."

"Well, yeah, but we all are," Tiff said. "Nobody I know sleeps at night."

"You left your phone downstairs, and it's been . . . screaming." She held it out to Tiff.

"Oh," Tiff said, laughing a little. "Sorry." She threw aside her quilt, scooted over, and patted the bed. "Get in with me."

Ivy crawled in next to Tiff and pulled up the blanket. They lay in the dark, staring up at the ceiling, where the stuck-on stars glowed green from the moonlight.

Ivy had received a B– in the lit class she'd taken with Prof. Chester (*And that was me being pretty generous, to be honest,* he'd told Ivy as they'd taken a bath together).

Tiff read Nat's text. "I have to call Doc, Mom," she said. "Pronto."

"Don't be ridiculous," Ivy said. "Do you know what time it is?"

"Do we have a CB radio?" Tiff asked. "Do we even know what that is?"

· 34 ·

A truck driver—perhaps the very same trucker who'd possibly driven me off the road?—had been the first to hear Daisy on the CB radio that Thanksgiving night. *Miranda,* he'd heard among the chatter of the CB. *Desiree.* He knew the Miranda-and-Desiree books well, because he'd read them aloud to his kids. Though the woman's voice was soft, too soft, he concluded that what he was hearing must be *The Coffins of Little Hope.* He texted his son about it, and his son texted his sister even though she sat in the chair next to him at the dinner table. They then texted all their friends.

Doc stayed up all night that Thanksgiving, making calls, gathering information, disrupting sleep in a number of houses, determined to be the first to report any news of a leak of parts of the forthcoming eleventh book, even if the leak had originated with his own printing plant. I couldn't sleep that night either. When Tiff and Ivy, in their coats and pajamas and winter boots, walked to Doc's house across the street, I was standing at my window naked, in the dark of the den, sipping hot bourbon and watching the snow. My white hair, full of knots and frizz, hung long and undone down my back. If anyone had been able to see in, they would've thought they'd seen a ghost.

After my run-in with the truck hours before, I'd arrived at Ivy's house and spoken not a word of the incident. I had nibbled at Ivy's unappetizing feast, careful not to let my still-jittering hand clink the fork against the plate.

"How *was* Lydie doing?" they'd asked.

"Oh, she was here and there," I'd said. Ivy had mulled the wine, and I'd stirred and stirred it with a cinnamon stick.

So upon arriving back at my house after dark, I'd stripped naked only because I could, because I could pace through my own rooms without anyone thinking I'd gone batty, without anyone rushing after me to cover me up. One normally doesn't think of being naked as a privilege, but it really is, I suppose, when your beauty and privacy have left forever. On the interstate, on the drive to the nursing home, I'd been passed by a young man on a motorcycle. Though the day had been cold, he'd worn no coat, and the wind had lifted his T-shirt, exposing his skin. That naked patch of flesh had seemed so tender, so in danger from any scrap of highway shrapnel, and I'd stared, captured by his skin's startling vulnerability.

But when I saw Tiff coming back out of Doc's house and walking across the street to mine, I put on my fur coat to answer the door. I waited a bit after she rang the bell so she wouldn't know I'd been up and rattling around so very late in the night.

"Do you have a CB radio?" Tiff asked.

"Why are you whispering?"

"Because it's night," she said.

"Why do you want a CB radio?" I asked.

Tiff affectionately petted the sleeve of my fur coat. "We should release Trudy back into the wild," she said.

"Trudy's much too old and mangy," I said. "She'd just be the day's kill for some stylish leopard-print coat. Why do you want a CB radio?"

"If you tell me that you have one, I'll tell you why I want one."

I didn't have one, but she told me anyway, and I slipped my feet into my slippers, buttoned my coat up as far as it would go, and followed Tiff to Doc's car. The stepmother of Tiff's friend Lucas drove a semitruck, and we were all off to cram ourselves into the cab to see what we could hear.

Which was nothing, as it turned out. Doc sat in the driver's seat fiddling with the CB radio's knobs, Tiff and I in the truck's sleeper, ears peeled for any suggestive bit of static.

I shivered and pulled my coat tighter around me. "What are you wearing under there, Great-Granny?" Tiff asked. "Some flimsy nightie?"

"Guess again," I said. "Something even flimsier."

"Like what?"

"Like nothing," I said.

"You're naked?" Tiff whispered. "What's wrong with you? Is Lydie's Alzheimer's contagious?"

"I don't know if I even believe in Lydie's Alzheimer's," I said. Tiff tugged on a loose red thread in the embroidery of my slipper, quickly undoing the petals of a rose. I slapped Tiff's hand away.

Pauline Creechly, a portly forty-something who wrote articles for Doc, arrived at the semitruck in a trench coat and stocking cap. On first sight, you might think chubby Pauline, with her pin curls and holiday sweaters, capable only of a homemaker's advice column, but she was a master of the redneck felony story, bringing a brisk, gum-chomping attitude to every local tale of domestic violence and trailer-park dog-fighting. "Whoever it is has been off the air for over an hour now,"

160

Pauline said, flipping open her notepad with an affected snap. "But I chatted with some folks who heard it. They told me the story—it sounds particularly morbid. If it's really *The Coffins of Little Hope*, Wilton Muscatine was in a pretty crappy mood when he wrote it. But here's the interesting part—Roy at the truck stop said it sounded like Daisy's voice. Our girl Daisy may be indulging in some serious copyright infringement."

"Beautiful," Tiff mumbled.

Part

· 35 ·

Daisy began reading chapter two on the Friday after Thanksgiving. Doc had bought a CB radio from a junk shop in the next county over and positioned it atop his dashboard—the radio had a tricky dial, and its cracked speaker hissed with every sibilant, but considering Daisy's hushed, listless delivery, we weren't missing much. Everyone was left to guess the specifics of at least half of what she read aloud. We parked as close as we could to the Crippled Eighty, but word had already widely spread of this potential unofficial leak, this illegal, inexpert performance of a book still two weeks from release, and hundreds of the impatient had driven, some for miles, to be within range of her frequency, to be the first to know what they could of Miranda and Desiree's plight.

We found ourselves—Doc and Tiff sitting in the front seat of Doc's car, Ivy and I in the back—piecing the story together from snippets of the heard and the misheard. Doc would hear Daisy say *the undertaker* while Tiff would hear *the undertow;* Ivy heard something about *bones in a butterfly net* while I heard something about *bends in a bubbling creek. Nettles in Miranda's lace* may have been *needles in her face,* depending on your sense of the book's sinister intent. In Doc's car, we listened and debated.

"False," Tiff said, hugging a pillow. She wore her pajamas beneath her parka. "Miranda and Desiree are not *gigglers*."

"I don't know," Ivy said. She sipped cold mulled wine from a lidded cup. "I could imagine those girls giggling over something. But I thought she said they were *sniffling, not giggling*."

"Shush," I said.

All the transcripts that listeners later posted online varied in marked ways, and podcasts recorded from the original CB broadcasts were mostly unlistenable, Daisy's voice too muted, the static too distracting.

"The end of chapter two," Daisy finally read. Only a moment of silence passed before the people in the cars up and down the road honked their horns and flashed their lights, a spontaneous gesture of community. *We all heard it,* we all seemed to be saying. *We all were there.*

"This is vintage Muscatine," Ivy said.

"I don't know, Sis," Doc said. "Maybe, maybe not. Sounds kind of authentic, but a little . . . I don't know . . . optimistic. But maybe writing the final book made him sentimental."

"It's fake," Tiff said, sighing to demonstrate her boredom. She breathed on the glass of the window and wrote "fake" backward in the fog, for anyone who might pass by.

They fancied themselves slavish experts; Doc

had been reading the Miranda-and-Desirees to Tiff since she was seven years old. He'd read some of them to her three or four times. They'd performed their own original theatricals with Tiff's Miranda and Desiree puppets, and they'd played the video game Miranda and Desiree's Medical Atrocities until their fingers had blistered.

We remained parked in the road as the other cars dispersed, and then Doc drove to the chained and padlocked front gate of the Crippled Eighty. Doc knew of a broken slat in a section of fence behind the fir trees, so we all followed him through the ditch and up onto the property. As we waited on the porch, Ivy helped me pluck off the sandburs that had stuck to my socks and pricked my skin. No Lenorians any longer attended to Daisy, and though the house's lamps were lit, we could see Daisy nowhere when we looked in the windows.

Even after we all agreed to give up after several rings of the bell and knocks on the door, Doc lingered. "She has an obligation," Doc said. "If she has a copy of *Coffins*, then she stole it. From me, from the printing press. When she was in my employ. She's required to surrender it."

"I agree with him," Tiff said. She no longer seemed bored now that confiscating the book had been suggested.

"What if Henceforth Books sues me?" Doc said.

"Why would they?" I said, though I knew that

Henceforth was quite litigious. Just a few days before, a holiday festival in North Dakota had featured snow-and-ice sculptures in a park for which an artist had illegally appropriated the illustrator's representation of Miranda and Desiree in the sixth book, a popular image of them in thin coats in a cold winter, their umbrellas spindly and threadbare as they glance back over their shoulders at the frostbiting storm on its way. Though the sculpture, due to an unseasonal massacre of Indian summer, had quickly melted down to just Miranda's and Desiree's flea-bitten legs, Henceforth Books had commanded a legal blitzkrieg on the violators. Over the years, Henceforth had shut down fan-based magazines and websites, unauthorized encyclopedias, unlicensed satire.

Despite Doc's anxiety, I still said not a word about my secret pen pal, but I stayed up late that night composing a plea to Muscatine. I begged him to ignore us. We could barely hear Daisy, I told him, so there was hardly any need to shut her up. We'd all lose interest quickly enough, I promised.

I finished my letter to Muscatine around 2 A.M. and only then noticed the noise of the wind rattling the glass in the windows of my house's front room. When was it, exactly, that I'd finally become used to quiet again? When I'd been widowed, the second time around, five years before, I'd kept some kind of racket always within earshot of every room of the house—TV, radio, records playing. I've never had any interest in tennis, but I came to be comforted by its announcers' hush and the rhythmic *thump* and volley of the ball.

I buttoned my sweater and put on my slippers to take the letter to the mailbox; I didn't want to risk oversleeping and missing the postman's early arrival. With one hand atop my head to keep my braids from wrecking and blowing in my face, the other clutching the envelope, I hurried to the end of the walk. When Tiff had lived across the street, I'd loved glancing up to her window in the middle of the night, where her lamp often still glowed behind the lowered blind.

After shutting the letter up tight in the mailbox and lifting the flag, I thought I could hear an old song above the whistle of the wind. Or maybe I was hearing it *in* the whistle of the wind, inventing the sound from something heard long ago. My skirt flapped once, with the hard, sharp snap of a sheet on a line, knocking the thread of the tune from my hearing. I walked back into the house and sat in the front hall in the little chair embroidered with birds with posies in their beaks, where Tiff would sit to put on and take off her winter boots before coming in or going out. I closed my eyes and tried to locate the song again. Even when I'd been young, I hadn't thought the popular songs were meant for me. I'd not been all that pretty, and clothes had so rarely flattered me. The songs, the fashions, they'd always been for other girls. They'd always been for the girls who knew by heart all the different dances.

· 36 ·

My letter to Muscatine crossed his in the mail, his arriving on Monday morning with no mention of Daisy at all.

I write this = Thanksgvn nite, he began. *Plez forgive = sentimentl.*

Muscatine wrote in fragments, in a rushed staccato of abbreviations and shorthand, but in between the dots and dashes—and even, in a way, because of them—I could intuit his anxiety, and an entire domestic scene unfolded before me. Wilton Muscatine was confiding in *me.* I stood next to the floor lamp in the parlor, the paper close to the bulb for the best light, and I squinted, translating.

He assumed, rightly, that I knew from tabloids certain details of his personal life. Muscatine had been married once briefly to a widow with a young girl, and though the widow now lived in Muscatine's Aspen chalet, which she'd wrestled away from him in a divorce, he still considered her daughter his own. Vanessa was now a recent college dropout. She proudly identified herself as homeless.

She'd taken to wearing vintage T-shirts and jeans of recycled denim. She devoted herself to environmental missions—some were as innocuous as righting turtles that had flipped onto their backs on a beach, while some were dangerous, such as hammering penny nails into trees so that loggers would wreck their saws.

"Come home," Muscatine told Vanessa, politely, "and stay home, why don't you." They sat at opposite ends of the long dining room table in Muscatine's home in Brooklyn, New York, a corner brownstone of blood-red brick with gables and a widow's walk up among its chimney pots. Muscatine had cooked their Thanksgiving dinner himself, though he'd been uncertain whether she'd even show up. Vanessa ate nothing of his turkey dinner, however; she'd brought her own bag of carrots she'd grown.

The maid served what looked to be a deep black tea.

"You'll drink tea, at least?" Muscatine said.

"Vile," Vanessa said after taking one sip. "Blech."

"It's not tea at all," Muscatine said, chuckling. "It's the ink used in the printing of *The Coffins of Little Hope*. The book is friendly to the environment. It's a vegetable-based ink; you can drink it, obviously. And the paper is made of garlic and coffee chaff."

"Your books, so far, have killed eight million trees," Vanessa said.

"Yes," he said, "yes, yes, yes," his voice drifting down with each *yes*. Though he'd been bald for decades now, he still had the habit, from when he'd worn his hair long, of reaching up to tuck it behind his ear. "It's all part of my diabolical plan," he said. "By cutting down the trees, I'm depleting the world of oxygen. And the people in their dizziness, deprived of oxygen, buy more of my books."

"Very funny," Vanessa said, not amused.

"If you're going to fret over the death of every living thing, Vanessa, you might as well kill yourself," he said. "Every time you scratch your nose you're committing a kind of microbial genocide. Parasites live on your skin. Bugs are squashed beneath your shoes. The only answer is to do yourself in and feed the earth. Before you kill again." But then he said, "I'm sorry for saying that. For suggesting that you kill yourself. I love you dearly. I never want to lose you."

"I'm in love," Vanessa said.

"No, you're not," Muscatine whispered.

"I can't hear you," she said.

"I said, 'No, you're not.'"

"She's famous in her field," Vanessa said. "She's in South America right now, helping pygmy lizards across a highway so they can tunnel in the sand."

"My goodness. She must be like a Christ figure to those lizards."

Muscatine had discussed with Henceforth Books publishing *Coffins* only electronically, to please his daughter. But even had Henceforth agreed to something so ridiculous, he knew Vanessa would've been just as disappointed in him. Though an electronic book was as thin as ether, to spark to life it required a plug into a plug into a plug, all funneling out to massive amounts of machinery that required fuels and the likely destruction of nests, streams, and entire habitats.

Ultimately, Muscatine allowed no electronic distribution of his books. It was too risky, he thought. No one, apparently, respected authorship anymore. Children were raised stealing music with music-stealing devices. They copied; they pasted. We'd created a nation of thieves by making everything so easy to lift. *Congratulations, greedy bastards! You've figured out a way to pillage the culture of its songs and stories and beauty, just as you pillaged nature of its flora and fauna.* We were out there, millions of us, every minute, with our virtual butterfly nets, decimating the garden sky of the pretty winged bugs so we could pin them to our walls to collect our dust.

"The book's paper is handmade and flecked with wildflower seeds," Muscatine said. He'd even worked the act of planting the book into the plot. Not only would *Coffins*, when buried, return its fibers to the earth, but it would engage a community of children with a creative act of conservation.

But Vanessa would not be moved by his efforts, which had come at considerable cost and negotiation—his demands for the greening of the book had doubled its retail price.

The maid brought Muscatine his advance copy of *The Coffins of Little Hope*, the smell of it that of cut dandelions and a burned cinnamon roll. He slid it along the tabletop toward Vanessa, nearly tipping over the gravy boat.

"The book is like something living," he told her. "You can't lose yourself in it. The paper's too scratchy and noisy, asserting itself. And its stitches could give long before you've reached the end."

"I'm happy for you," she said.

"You sound weary," he said hopefully. Perhaps, he thought, she was disappointed in the choices she'd made. "Come home, Vanessa," he said.

"We're saving bats from wind power," she said. "Those tall wind turbines in the fields are blowing them up. Air flows over the turbine blades, and the bats' little lungs go *pop*. We've been following convoys of trucks that are hauling the blades for new turbines, and we're sneaking sugar into their gas tanks."

"Let me join you, then," he said. "I could help. I'm just sick to my stomach about those exploding bats, now that I've heard about them."

"You'd hate it," she mumbled. "There's no chance at success. And people like you aren't happy with anything less than everything."

"Did someone tell you to say that to me?" he said. "Your girlfriend, maybe?"

"Nice, Pops," she said, crunching the last of her carrots and standing from the table. She raised her voice, and she picked up the napkin that had been folded into a swan, just so she could shake it apart from its elegant folds and toss it haughtily back onto the table. "I'm not smart enough, am I, to say what I mean when there's something meaningful . . . something meaningful that I'm saying to you?"

Muscatine stood. They both stayed standing, still, at opposite ends of the table. "I mean, Vanessa, that you're too smart to need someone telling you how to speak to me. You're the only person in the world who knows me at all."

"Who *doesn't* know you?" Vanessa said, practically yelling now, the squeak of her higher notes causing in Muscatine a fit of nostalgia, reminding him of when she'd been fourteen, back when he'd still been able to convince himself she'd someday outgrow her frustrations. "Your fame has killed eight—"

"Yes," he interrupted, "eight million, eight million trees. I know, I know." He didn't think it the time to remind her that he'd also saved lives. In the fifth book, he'd described so expertly how to build a mechanical heart so tiny that it could be placed in an unborn infant that it had been used as a blueprint for the invention of a device that had rescued hundreds of preemies around the world. "The Heart of Dizzy Soozie," the device had been named, after the heartsick fetus in the book.

Vanessa left before pumpkin pie. In the evening, Muscatine took his new book into the garden behind the house—he'd had the advance copy for a few weeks but had yet to examine it. He sat in a creaking wooden chair among the dried-up tomato vines in their cages. He pressed the book against his knees, opened the cover, and tore out the book's pages, page by page, starting with the dedication *(To my daughter, Vanessa)*, dropping the paper into the dirt and letting the wind carry it up into the twisting thicket of branches he'd braided together when the trees had been young.

· *37* ·

One of us died that Thanksgiving weekend—one of us death merchants, that is. Mrs. Oliver, the owner of Mrs. Oliver's, a men's and women's clothing store, had been nearly twenty years younger than me. Nonetheless, I'd always called her *Mrs.* Oliver, just as everyone else had, just as we'd all called her mother-in-law *Mrs.* when she'd been alive and had run the shop. At Mrs. Oliver's, an institution on the town square, we could always rely upon a hasty turnaround on the tailoring of a suit in disrepair or a favorite dress that had grown too tight, so we could either attend a fast-approaching funeral or, more grimly, be the funeral's guest of honor. Rarely would you go to Mrs. Oliver's for something kicky—aside from a few tropical shirts in the summertime or some pastels at Easter, the shop was a somber affair, rack after rack of variations on gray and navy and wine.

I attend many funerals, as do many of the death merchants, and we all lurk in a back pew, in black and feathers, perched like carrion. Mrs. Oliver had always been the one among us who'd cried, so as we sat so dry-eyed at her funeral that Tuesday, we were nearly moved to tears by our own lack of emotion. We'd loved Mrs. Oliver, to be sure, and we would miss her; she had died before even seeing her seventies. But so many of the ceremonies in this German-American community, by their very design, did what they could to deaden. The eulogies given by all the town's ministers tended to be impersonal and condemning, reminding us again and again that it was our own sin that assured our demise— mortality was a human invention, it seemed. We'd received our death sentence long before our birth.

At the crowded Garden of Gethsemane Lutheran Church, we tucked ourselves into the nursery at the back, in a short pew among a few cribs and a playpen, a window of glass between us and the mourners, the sermon piped in through speakers. A sprawled rag doll had lain on the pew, its skirt tossed up over its head. I kept it on my lap throughout the service, plucking lint from the black yarn of its hair.

When Mrs. Oliver's nephew, a man with a waxed mustache, sang the Lord's Prayer with the nasal-tinged warble of a barbershop quartet, his "power" and his "glory," though up from deep in his lungs, were about as powerful and glorious as the yodel of a toad.

Loraleen Griffen, who sold tombstones and carried with her always a cloud of Chanel, wiggled her skinny butt in next to me. "I was running late," she whispered, the funeral nearly over but for the reverend's "go forth in peace." What people tended to remember of Loraleen was not her salesmanship but rather the fingernails she tapped at her catalogs with—rose-colored nails an impractical two inches long. It was impossible for anyone, even those deepest in grief, not to comment on them, which Loraleen always took as a compliment. "What was she wearing?" Loraleen asked.

"They put her in the burgundy," I said. "And with the gold scarf."

"Oh, of course, of course," Loraleen said. "How was her coloring?"

"Not so hot," I said. "She'd been sick for so

many months. Rouge can only restore so much vitality."

Loraleen took her compact from her purse to do a quick check of the red of her lipstick. She had never shopped at Mrs. Oliver's—she wore to the funeral an ivory-colored pantsuit and a pair of peacock-blue pumps.

"Is this what you guys do?" Doc asked me, whispering in my ear. "Heckle the dead?" Doc despised funerals, but he'd dated Mrs. Oliver's daughter, Hailey, in high school, and hoped to demonstrate by his presence his sympathetic nature now that she was newly divorced.

"Shhh," I said. "You don't get to talk during the funeral." But it was true—we in the nursery pew did consider ourselves excused from sobriety. We were the ones who allowed these mere mortals to commemorate their dead. We told their stories, cleaned them and clothed them, manicured their nails and repaired their damages. We accepted death, numbed ourselves to its decay, so they didn't have to—so they didn't have to endure anything more morbid than some wilted flowers and days of grief.

The coin, I thought with a gasp that Doc noticed. He raised his shoulders and furrowed his brow with question. I shook my head. "Nothing," I said, but my heart was rapid. It had been my turn to secretly drop the coin in the casket, a tradition among us waxworks in the back pew. Mrs. Oliver had even been the one to start it. *How awful of me,* I thought. But it wasn't too late, perhaps—the funeral director was one of us. He'd surely lift the lid for me. I reached into my coat pocket and ran my fingers along the penny's edge.

After Loraleen's sculptor had died several years before—he'd carved hundreds and hundreds of names and roses and crosses into granite—we'd gathered at the tavern to toast him with buttered rum in copper cups. We had tried out on each other our own possible epitaphs—I proposed I be buried beneath a filthy limerick, and Morty, our town's estate lawyer, had proclaimed that he wanted to be memorialized as "Captain of the Stygian Ferry." He'd then explained that, in myth, one had to pay the ferryman to cross the River Styx into the Underworld. Ancient peoples had been buried with coins in their mouths for the fare.

"To *us*," Mrs. Oliver had toasted, raising her cup to all at the table. She'd been so plump then, and always so worried over her weight, experimenting with every fad diet and new brand of caffeine pill. "To us, the ferrymen." And the name caught on, as did Mrs. Oliver's suggestion that we establish our own eccentric ritual of dropping a penny into each casket at every funeral we attended, as our private gift to the deceased.

The organist began her recessional, and Mrs. Oliver's family stood to be ushered down the aisle. "Hailey's ex-husband didn't even come,"

Doc whispered to me as Hailey Oliver, her little girl holding her hand, stepped down the aisle.

"That's the beauty of an ugly divorce," I said. "You no longer have to attend to each other's needs." Doc had been married once, at twenty-two, for three years, to, literally, a farmer's daughter, and just like all those farmers' daughters in that genre of dirty jokes, she'd been distressingly hot-to-trot.

Doc's wife had had a job driving from town to town with a van full of stuffed animals and plastic jewelry, and she'd gone from restaurant to movie theater to game hall filling those arcade machines—the ones in which you operate the tiny jaws of a jittery crane and attempt to snatch up a worthless prize. She'd had a weakness, particularly, for bartenders—the grislier the tattoos, the better. She'd liked it rough, it seemed, and she'd come home to my gentle grandson, after just a few days on the road, with provocative cuts and bruises, and she would cry and confess and give Doc gifts of poly-filled pandas with blue-glass eyes.

Doc had not even kicked her out—she'd had the nerve to leave *him,* for a penniless, celibate folk singer she'd met at a county fair. Not only would the singer not beat her, he wouldn't touch her, but somehow she was in love like she'd never been before. She and the folk singer are still married.

So Doc, depleted as some men get when a

woman proves ghastly, had committed himself to the newspaper, then eventually to Tiff, and dated only every now and again. So I'd been pleased to see Hailey Oliver walking with only her daughter, the ex, apparently, completely out of the picture.

Coffee brewing at a funeral smells different than coffee brewing anywhere else. You don't even have to drink it to receive its full restorative effects—the frugal church volunteers reuse the grounds, adding a few spoonfuls of fresh to the soggy filter. I've been a volunteer myself for so many years, I can't resist assisting even when I'm not on the committee—so as Doc sat with the ferrymen enjoying some egg salad and crumb cake, I went around the fellowship hall with a carafe, refilling cups.

"Do you take your coffee black, Pipsqueak?" I asked Hailey Oliver's daughter—a five-year-old with thick spectacles consuming her face. I suspect Hailey thought me senile, for she put her hand over her daughter's cup of lemonade.

"She only drinks Sanka," Hailey said, winking.

I'd written Mrs. Oliver's obit over the weekend, or rather, I'd polished it up, having plucked it nearly complete from the Impending Doom file. Mrs. Oliver's condition had been terminal for so long that we'd almost become suspicious. For the obit I had spoken only with Mrs. Oliver's son, a local dentist, so I introduced myself to Hailey as Doc's grandmother, calling Doc by his given name, Eugene, since his nickname had not evolved until after he'd gone to work for the newspaper. I'd been tempted to call him her high school sweetheart as well, but that would have embarrassed Doc even if it were true, and it certainly wasn't at all; he and Hailey had gone on just a handful of uneventful dates. She'd actually met her true high school sweetheart the year after she'd dated Doc, and she'd married him, and they'd moved to Omaha, and they were now embroiled in a separation even more passionate than their love affair had ever been.

"I haven't seen Eugene in so long," Hailey said. "How is he doing?"

"He can speak for himself," I said, and I gestured for Doc to come over.

"He's here?" Hailey said. She stood, and as Doc approached, she seemed genuinely overtaken. She hugged him, then stepped back to look at his face, putting her hands to his cheeks. "Just look at you," she said. "It suits you, the hair that's going away. You have a good forehead for it."

"You look exactly the same," he said, though I didn't think so, and he probably didn't either. She was Doc's age—thirty-eight—but she looked older than that. She'd been a little chubby in high school, and like her mother, she'd been often hopped up on diet pills. She was now terribly thin in a way that didn't seem deliberate. Maybe the divorce had been a long time coming.

Doc and Hailey sat to talk, and Hailey introduced him to Sibyl, her little girl with the old-lady name. "Nobody really calls me Eugene anymore, thank God," he said. "They call me Doc now." Sibyl offered him some of the candy corn in her paper bag.

"Eat at your own risk," Hailey said. "It's left over from Halloween. Sibyl likes it stale."

"Are you a doctor like Dr. Vince?" Sibyl asked.

"I'm not a real doctor," Doc said.

"Neither is Dr. Vince, really," Hailey said. "He's Sibyl's acupuncturist back in Omaha."

"Sibyl has an acupuncturist?"

"Well, she has lots of doctors, don't you, sweetie?" Hailey said, and Sibyl nodded. "You know," Hailey said, eating some candy corn, "when Sibyl was at the hospital for her tonsillectomy, we coached her to ask her doctor, told her to do that joke, where she asks, 'Hey, Doc, will I be able to play the piano after my surgery?' so he'd say, 'Of course,' and then she could say, 'That's funny, I was never able to play the piano *before*,' which she thought was just witty as hell, though I don't know that she really fully got it, since she was only four, but anyway, she did it, she asked the doctor, 'Will I be able to play the piano after my tonsils get yanked out?' and the doctor, he says, 'Only if you could play the piano before the surgery.' Can you believe that? He had to have known he was being set up for the joke, but he couldn't let her have that moment? I mean, I realize doctors probably get tired of that joke, but why should he value his opportunity to stomp on her punch line more than the opportunity to let a sick little girl get a laugh from the couple of nurses standing there? *He* got the laugh instead—a polite, embarrassed little bit of twittering from the nurses."

"Well, he probably looked like a jerk to the nurses too, if that's any consolation," Doc said. He popped some candy corn into his mouth.

"She's a real little hothouse flower, this one," Hailey said, tucking a hank of Sibyl's hair behind her ear.

· *38* ·

What's it mean when somebody says somebody's a hothouse flower?" Doc asked us that evening as we awaited Daisy's hypnotic monotone. He took off a mitten and skimmed his fingertip over the top of the wine in his glass to gather up a speck of something.

Doc had moved the CB radio from the car and installed it in the house. The wind had picked up both outside and inside, winter wanting to settle in good and fierce, and we sipped the leftover mulled wine that Ivy had brought over and reheated in a saucepan. Doc's house was a Cape Cod cast adrift far from sea, and we'd all always adored it even as we cursed its chill and Doc's indifference to the icicles that often formed on the edges of windowpanes. It wasn't that he was hot-blooded; he just didn't mind being cold.

"Buxom?" Ivy said. "Is that what it means? Or maybe I'm thinking of a hothouse *tomato*."

I nibbled off the limbs of a gingerbread man, pushing my woolen scarf down off my lips and chin to take each bite. "Delicate," I said.

"You remember Hailey Oliver?" Doc asked.

"No," Ivy said without hesitation.

"Don't be ridiculous," he said. "You both were in plays in high school. And junior high. I think you even played sisters once. In *One Flew over the Cuckoo's Nest* or something."

"*You* don't be ridiculous," she said, sighing, rubbing her neck as if wearied by the conversation. "There are no sisters in *Cuckoo's Nest*."

"You were *hookers*," I said. Why do these young ones remember so little of their own lives? "The girl with the terrible lisp somehow got the part of Nurse Ratched, and nobody could understand a word she said. It was a long night. Hailey Oliver played a hooker, and you played another hooker."

"No," Ivy said, "*I* played the hooker, and *she* played the other hooker."

"So you do remember," Doc said. "You said you didn't remember."

"You didn't believe me anyway, so what does it matter?"

"But why wouldn't you just say you remembered her when I asked you if you remembered her?"

"If you were so sure I remembered her," Ivy said, "then why'd you ask to begin with?"

"Hey, shhhh, shut up," Tiff said, but she said it gently, looking up from her book.

"Your Uncle Doc and I aren't fighting, honey," Ivy said.

"No, I mean, shut up and listen," Tiff said. We all tried to hear past the quiet of the room until we realized it was the quiet we were listening for. "She's like a half hour late," Tiff said.

Doc jiggled the wires and knobs of the CB as Tiff texted friends. No one's CB anywhere was picking up Daisy, it seemed. Another hour passed: more mulled wine, more wind rattling the panes.

"There you have it," Tiff finally said. "A fraud. She's got nothing left." She walked to the Christmas tree in the corner and clucked her tongue and shook her head, disappointed in Doc's arrangement. Doc had never bought an ornament in his adult life—ever since his parents had died, he'd decorated only with the ornaments of his childhood. Tiff moved a long-legged elf from a lower branch to an upper one. She relocated a crocheted snowman of unraveling yarn. She pinched the silk gown of an angel hanging crookedly from a hook in her left wing, lifting the skirts to reveal porcelain joints hinged with old twine.

"The French don't put up trees," Ivy said.

"Yeah, you've said that," Tiff said. All week Ivy had been educating us in French tradition, but when Tiff had gone online to investigate Ivy's gratingly European approach to decorating—slippers full of chestnuts instead of stockings on the hearth, birds of spun sugar on the windowsill—she'd found pictures of a holiday gaudy like our own, trees included.

Tiff wandered off into what we called the sunroom, though the overgrown maple trees thick in the backyard kept all the sun out, even in the winter, when the branches were bare. She shut the door behind her, closing herself off from the rest of us. Coats hung from hooks near the door that led outside, but the coats were for inside, for the sunroom, which was bitterly cold until March. Tiff put on a parka and dropped into the creaking easy chair in the corner, where she usually sat to read, and plucked at the pills of lint in the chair's fabric. She'd heard of people sacrificing heat in their homes for reasons both spiritual and environmental. Maybe, she considered, she'd move out of Ivy's house and into this frigid sunroom, where she'd fashion a makeshift yurt from bookcases and sleep nearly crushed beneath heavy quilts. She would locate a cosmic peace.

Tiff wasn't sure why she was so antsy to hear

Daisy read more of her rendition of *Coffins*, especially because she was convinced of its inauthenticity. Tiff had read online far more convincing rip-offs and had even once tried her own hand at fan fiction—she'd posted, to an unauthorized Miranda-and-Desiree website, a short story about an orphaned wolf-girl who devoured the rabbits that decimated the vegetable gardens of Rothgutt's Asylum. Tiff knew of some pieces of Miranda-and-Desiree fan fiction that had become legendary in their own right, stories widely and covertly exchanged. There was even fan fiction derived from fan fiction, unofficial plotlines and characters and threads growing like weedy infestations.

Tiff pulled her arms up out of the sleeves of the parka and brought her hands in close to her chest, folding them prayer-like over her heart, feeling for her heart's thump; she took delight in the rapid chattering of her teeth, as if the cold room were some kind of amusement-park ride. She thought about all the different lives she'd already led, and the different lives she could yet lead, lives that perhaps would better reflect her personality. Maybe she could become famous as the yurt girl of Nebraska, then famous again later when everyone wondered whatever happened to her.

Tiff went to the bookcase along the wall, poked her arms back through the sleeves of the parka, and reached up to tug at the corner of the spine of a book on the top shelf. It was a hollowed-out copy of the third Miranda-and-Desiree book, *The Key to the Hollowed-Out Book*, that Doc had bought for Tiff at a craft fair; a guy with a jigsaw had sliced out the book's insides and fitted it with hinges. The heart-shaped lock had long since ceased to clasp, and Tiff had lost the key long before that. Kept inside were notes Tiff had once thought significant, little slips of paper passed between the girls in school, notes full of confessions of love for this boy or that one, notes demanding apologies, notes full of lies meant to incite gossip. It made Tiff cringe to read them now. Though the oldest were from only a few years before, it embarrassed her that she'd felt so strongly about things so dumb. So what if Aubrey had sat next to Lucas at lunch? And who cared that Cecily had picked Sara last for kickball in gym class? But Tiff couldn't resist returning to the notes again and again, revisiting old anxieties that had grown weak and silly.

Tiff put the hollowed-out book back on the shelf, took down the tenth book, and returned to her chair to thumb through it. She couldn't imagine reading *The Coffins of Little Hope* anywhere else than in this cold room of Doc's, wearing a pair of gloves from which she'd cut off half of each finger and drinking hot cocoa from a soup mug. Tiff suspected her doubts about Daisy's *Coffins* rose from the fact that it wasn't a book at all, no matter who had written it. Tiff needed the words on the page to become the voice in her head, her own voice, or an approximation of it, and she needed the paper and the sound of the scratch of her chapped fingertips against it as she fiddled with each page, ever ready to turn it.

· *39* ·

Daisy never did read that evening. She had somehow sneaked unseen from her house and pushed her bike across the field, away from the road where the rows of cars parked, over the rise and fall of the hills of the Crippled Eighty. She walked alongside mulberry trees her father had years before planted at the edge of the property as windbreaks. Daisy, as a girl, had gone out there with her mother in the summer to pick the berries; they'd wear light sundresses and sip Tab from straws stuck in bottles, and they'd lay a sheet beneath the trees and shake the branches to collect the berries. Daisy had always eaten most of them on the walk back, the fruit sweet on sour stems.

Daisy now walked into the wind, into a slight snowfall that stung her skin. She wore an old parka, its hood up, but she hadn't been able to find her gloves. She pushed the bike with one hand on one handle, the other hand in her pocket, switching sides as her fingers froze up. Slung across her arm was a satchel.

In the bare trees still hung plastic owls her father had attached to the branches to startle the crows. The owls, dented and broken, hung crookedly on rope, the paint of their yellow eyes long since washed away by rain. Crows nested there now, next to the spinning owls.

"A *murder* of crows," Daisy had said to her father one winter, a few days after her mother had left for good. Daisy had graduated from high school the spring before. She had sat smoking a cigarette next to a window open a crack.

"A flock," her father said, looking out the window with her, up to where the birds crossed the gray winter sky.

"I read in a book that it was a murder," she said.

"In the books *you* read, maybe," he said. He took her cigarette from her for a drag off it. "But it's just a flock. A flock of birds." They'd migrated down across the Great Lakes from Canada, he explained, to winter in Nebraska trees. "But the ones who stay through summer are the very worst," he said, contemplative. In the summer, he said, they littered the stone birdbath in the garden with the carcasses of snakes and mice and the nestlings of songbirds.

Daisy had preferred to think of the birds with pretty red cherries in their beaks.

She led her bike past the mulberry trees and into

the forest of overgrown firs, then down a hill to a weather-wrecked fence. She lifted her bike up and over broken slats and walked across the neighboring field, the wheels following the plowed ruts in the hard ground. At the edge of a desolate road that led to a highway overpass, she pushed her bike up the side of the hill, the dried blossoms of musk thistle sticking to the fake fur of her hood's collar, the thistles' stems cracking beneath her tires. Once on the pavement, she rode, unnoticed, along the highway's shoulder for a mile or so to the Bon Voyage Motel. She rented a room with a roll of one-dollar bills.

· *40* ·

Daisy lifted from the vanity a tiny blue bottle of some plain-label eau de toilette. *Lilac Splash* was the scent. She put the bottle back without opening it, exactly as she'd found it, on a tray of lotions, bubble bath, toothpaste. She took only a plastic comb from the tray so she could run it through her hair, damp from the wet wind and snow. Her skin raw and numb, tingling as if from needles, she longed to soak in a hot bath and to curl up in the warm sheets for a nap.

She sat, strumming her thumb over the teeth of the comb, on a straight-backed chair pulled up close to the TV, her knees against the TV table, waiting for the episode of *Missing in America* that had been filmed in our town weeks before.

There'd never been a TV at the Crippled Eighty. Her father had sometimes listened to the AM radio, to weather bulletins during thunderstorms and to farm reports and to a lunchtime program called *Call-in for Cash*, in which the host spun a wheel, the wheel *clickety-click*ing fast, then slow, and if the letters matched your initials, you could win twenty dollars.

But even before Daisy's mother had left them, her father had spent evenings in the kitchen alone, at a desk with a CB radio, a home base, to chat with the truckers on the highway, filling the house with the low mutter of strangers only passing through. He would talk to them, get to know a thing or two about them, until their voices broke into pieces of half-heard words in the crackle of distance, and they were gone, often forever. Even after the CB had long fallen out of fashion, he remained committed to it as Daisy lost herself in novels, reading by the too-little light of a dim lamp.

We all watched *Missing in America* that night, but it had little to offer about Elvis. They hadn't even unearthed his real name. They showed the police sketch, and the Polaroid of Lenore, and a few of the aerial photographs Elvis had sold to area farmers. The show featured dramatizations and some interviews with women of nearby communities who'd invited Elvis into their homes when he'd stopped by to peddle his pictures.

"I've known child molesters all my life, and this man was not one," said a woman who held a shivering Chihuahua against the lace ruffles of her blouse.

They also showed clips of Daisy skulking about in her overgrown vegetable garden on the Crippled Eighty, grainy footage that resembled films of Bigfoot. They talked about her lately reading from *The Coffins of Little Hope*, and they showed outdated stock footage of a printing plant, page after page rolling off a tumbler with a roar of heavy machinery. "Daisy worked for a press that was secretly printing some of the copies of the latest Miranda-and-Desiree," the narrator said. "Was she able to sneak a copy out?"

Missing in America then cut to a commercial for some prescription drug that promised sleep and gentle dreams. Daisy thought of Elvis in her house one morning, days before he'd left, having his coffee at the kitchen sink, crabby from too little sleep, his lower lip stuck out, puffy, in a pout. She thought of the way he would kiss her passionately, then stop kissing to put his head at her neck, resting it there as he held her.

She turned off the TV but couldn't bring herself to go back out on her bike in the cold. She turned the TV back on, changing the channel to a rerun of an old sitcom, and sat in the chair for another half hour, running her thumb over the teeth of the comb again and again. One of the commercials advertised a drug that seemed appropriate for her, though she didn't know what it was or what it was for. It was a plum-colored tablet. In the first part of the ad, the woman sat in a room with the curtains drawn and the lights turned off, inches from a TV, its screen busy with commercial messages. By the end of the ad, the woman was tending to a rosebush, wearing a yellow dress with red polka dots, her hair springy with curls.

· 41 ·

Abby Most, the minister's wife, stopped for Daisy in the early morning. The sun had not yet come up, and Daisy peddled her bike slowly along the highway's shoulder. Abby was on her way to Grand Island to serve pancakes at a feed benefiting earthquake victims and had no way of knowing it was Daisy beneath the hood of the heavy parka.

Abby, as before, indulged Daisy's silence as they drove to the Crippled Eighty, the bicycle in the half-closed trunk, its wheels spinning with the bumps in the road.

"What's in the satchel?" Abby finally asked when they reached the farm.

Daisy clutched her satchel closer to her chest and began to cry. "I'm sorry," she said. "I didn't sleep. I'm catching a cold." Daisy then rambled on, nearly incoherent with all the sobbing, about her night in the motel. She told Abby Most about *Missing in America* and the commercials for the prescriptions she might need.

"Now, now," Abby said, purring the words. Abby put her hand on Daisy's, then moved her hand across the satchel's vinyl flap. "What's in the satchel?" Abby asked. "Is it the book? The eleventh book? Do you really have it?"

Daisy opened the satchel to show Abby a spiral-bound notebook, opening it, displaying its pages covered with a child-like handwriting that leaned back instead of forth—words so tight against each other that the ink turned the pages stiff and crinkly. Every inch of white was covered with tiny black words etched with a hard hand onto the page. "It's nothing," Daisy said. "It says nothing."

"You wrote this?" Abby asked. Abby had volunteered once with mentally disabled adults, and it had saddened her deeply to see the shivery, uneven scribbling of one of the men. It had looked as if he'd held the pencil in his fist. How dreadful to have even just your signature reveal so much turmoil. But then something occurred to Abby. Who, other than a childish adult, might write like a child? "Tell me the truth." Abby put her hand on Daisy's wrist. "You've always been able to tell me the truth. Daisy, did Lenore write this?"

Daisy sat without speaking, without crying, her

hair in her face. She seemed to be contemplating the question, but she didn't answer Abby. She returned the notebook to her satchel and stepped from the car. "Please don't tell anyone," Daisy said.

"Don't worry," Abby said, absently running her fingers along the blunt cut of her bangs. "Nobody listens to me."

Part

Whenever he was nervous, Doc drank Pepto, guzzled it practically, and as he did, he pictured the old ads from TV, the cartoon X-ray of a man's insides coated with a soothing, settling pink. As Doc sipped the Pepto direct from the bottle, I enjoyed a few swallows of dessert wine before dinner.

We were expecting company—Mrs. Oliver's daughter, Hailey, and Hailey's daughter, Sibyl. Doc had cranked the furnace to crisp things up. Chilled nonetheless, I kept my fur on, draped over my shoulders; Doc, however, seemed to be sweating. He would mop at his brow with the end of his necktie—not the necktie he'd worn to work but one he'd changed into.

Less than a week had passed since Abby Most had offered Daisy a ride, but the front-page headline of the International Weekly Wonder, a rag full of gossip and aliens and paparazzi shots of celebrities with fallen facelifts, announced, "Daisy Tells Minister's Wife: 'Lenore Wrote It.'" Doc had read aloud to me from the article, in which Abby Most described a red notebook, its pages filled with a frenzied cursive. Before Abby's eyes, a few words rose from the page: *Miranda, mother, asylum.* "I think she really wanted to confide in me," Abby had told the reporter. Daisy had alleged to Mrs. Most that Lenore had left her red notebook, her own version of *Coffins*, under a bed in the basement, where the girl had often hidden to write and draw. Daisy now read Lenore's story on the CB radio, simply seeking connection.

Meanwhile, Doc's latest edition of the County Paragraph had been far less newsworthy, featuring only a front-page story on Daisy's sniffles and sore throat. He swallowed another shot of Pepto. "I even dropped by Daisy's house that day," Doc said to me as he paced the living room. "Why didn't I demand to see what she's been reading from? All I did was fix her some soup. I'm not a newspaperman, Granny. I'm a social worker."

He was, truly, a bit of a hothouse flower, I thought.

"Why didn't Abby Most call *me* when she saw the notebook?" he said. "You have to respect the order of these kinds of things, don't you? You can't just be grabbing at headlines when you're coaxing a story along." The Pepto had turned his tongue black, and he wrung his hands as he spoke. "Daisy is telling me her own truth in her own time."

"Isn't this version of the story better?" I suggested. "You should be happy Daisy didn't steal a copy of the real book, shouldn't you? If she did, then she stole it from under *your* nose, from *your* printing press. And when you write about it all in the Paragraph, your newspaper could be said to be profiting from the theft." I'd honestly meant to be consoling, but when I saw Doc rubbing his temples and shaking his head, I added, "I'm only playing devil's advocate."

"We've profited from a lot of theft," he said. "That's what people read the newspaper *for*. Theft, corruption, murder. People can convince themselves they lead charmed lives if they can read about all the terrible fates they've avoided. In the newspaper business, your only real commodity is bad bad bad news." He pointed at me with his bottle of Pepto. "Where, for example, would an obit writer be without the public's morbid curiosity?"

Uninterested in defending my life's work, I raised my glass, nodded, winked. *Well said,* I didn't say. He'd spoken sharply and quickly, but I knew he wasn't angry. His feelings were hurt; he felt betrayed by both Daisy and Abby Most. Doc felt possessive of Lenore, I knew, but so did we all. In speaking to someone outside the community, Abby Most had spoken out of turn. But, of course, when it came right down to it, Abby Most had no responsibility to anyone but herself. One thing I've had to discover anew over and over again in my many, many years: a small town has only the *illusion* of a devoted and close-knit family. None of us are family. We are all deeply alien, one to the other.

Nonetheless, I suspected that in living rooms all across our town, the article on Daisy had been clipped and pasted into scrapbooks or slipped into plastic sleeves and tucked in drawers. I suspected it had become, instantly, a cherished relic of our town's notoriety. To have made the front page of the lowly International Weekly Wonder, a tabloid we all thumbed through as we waited in line at the supermarket checkout, was to have reached a kind of pinnacle.

"Have you spoken to Daisy about it?" I asked.

"No," he said. "I'm furious at her." A mirror hung above the fireplace, and he stopped to loosen the knot of his tie just so. Whenever he pictured himself, he never pictured himself quite so slouched. He never pictured his clothes fitting so poorly. "And she's had her phone disconnected. She couldn't bear how it never rang with news of Lenore."

He folded the International Weekly Wonder and tossed it into the hearth's flame.

· 43 ·

Ivy volunteered to cook that night and to bring her dishes and tureens to Doc's. She'd lately practiced a culinary sparseness, based on her obsolete cookbooks, that had been leaving us all hungry, our stomachs grumbling even as we ate. She probably thought she'd be impressing Hailey with our sophistication. Ivy brought along a tablecloth tatted with lace grapes, and some candles and pewter candlesticks, tugging the whole works behind her in a wicker doll pram. She leaned into the wind and snow, her umbrella blown nearly inside out, and she wore a poncho constructed from a Navajo blanket.

Ivy served us our salad last—a teensy dish of prickly weeds, slices of unpeeled pear, and pungent blue cheese—after a watery stew of canned chestnuts and a stringy bird meat bought from a neighbor who hunted game, a bird I suspected was nothing more exotic than the doves that cooed on the telephone wires. But Hailey seemed not to mind, and she seemed not to eat. She looked pretty in her satiny blue dress, a row of tiny cloth roses on the barrette in her hair. She wore her cardigan like a librarian might, with her arms out of the sleeves, the sleeves dangling at her sides, only the top button buttoned at the neck.

Tiff, always quick to get familiar, reached over to take Sibyl's glasses from her face. She tried them on, and a jolt of pain shot through her temples. She handed them back to the child. "You should get laser surgery on your eyeballs, Sib," Tiff said.

Hailey said, "I know a woman who got that surgery in one of those trailers that they park in mall parking lots, and now she sees ghosts all the time. Right out of the corner of her left eye."

Sibyl was five, almost the same age Tiff had been when Ivy had left her with Doc. *I probably looked just as pathetic,* Tiff thought. Sibyl had refused to remove her pink windbreaker with its zipper that stuck only halfway up its track. It depressed Tiff, this little girl all decked out like a ragamuffin at a bus stop. Even her tights had runs.

Hailey seemed to notice Tiff's scrutiny. "I had a pretty green velvet dress for Sibyl to wear tonight, but she only likes to wear the stuff she's already worn out," she said. "I shouldn't let her, I suppose. I'm an awful parent." She reached across the table to take Sibyl's hand. "They should take you away from me, shouldn't they, sweetie?"

Doc reached over to touch at a needle in the chignon knotted atop Hailey's head. "Is that needle doing something?" he asked.

"Oh," she said, surprised, reaching up to pluck it out. She dropped it into her empty coffee cup. "I'm full of pins." Hailey, an accomplished seamstress herself, had taken over the shop from her mother months before. She now began pulling pins from everywhere—another in her chignon, a few stuck in the hem of her dress. She dropped them all into her cup.

Ivy brought to the table a wiggly black cake on a china pedestal. "If Doc had any matches," she said, "I could've set the whole thing on fire for you. It's soaked in rum."

"Oh," Hailey said, going to her purse on a

corner chair. She took out a vinyl cigarette case with a little hook at its side for a lighter. As she handed the lighter to Ivy, she seemed to notice the polite indifference we were feigning. "Oh, I smoke hardly at all," she said. "Hardly ever. I'm quitting even as we speak. See?" She lifted up the short sleeve of her dress, with a quick, flirtatious peek-a-boo, to show Doc the nicotine patch on her upper arm, situated next to a tattoo of a thorny rose.

Ivy raised an eyebrow in Tiff's direction, then touched the lighter's flame to the cake's center. The cake went up with a *whoosh,* and we all, all but Tiff, applauded.

"Smells disgusting," Tiff said.

"Rude," Ivy said.

After Ivy extinguished the cake by blanketing it with a damp tea towel, she sliced it up, and we all grew silent, like clockwork. Eight o'clock had rolled around, and though Daisy had not been reading on the radio much over the last handful of evenings—and the one night she had, her voice had been so wispy with laryngitis that we hadn't made out a single word—we still listened closely for her voice, out of hope and newborn habit.

"Is Sibyl looking forward to *The Coffins of Little Hope* coming out next week?" Doc asked Hailey. "Does she like the Miranda-and-Desirees?"

"She probably would," Hailey said, "if I wasn't

such a fuddy-duddy. I'm afraid I don't approve." She spoke as if embarrassed by her moral stance. She toyed with a button of her sweater. "It's unsettling the delight we take in stories of endangered children, isn't it?" I could see Tiff bristle, see her sense a hint of accusation.

"Those flying monkeys in *The Wizard of Oz* still creep me out," Ivy said, pouring coffee.

"You hated the blueberry girl in Willy Wonka too," Doc said.

"I didn't hate the girl," Ivy said. "I hated what became of her."

I wondered if Doc was thinking of the book I'd given him when he'd been a little boy, a children's illustrated guide to magic, with advice on how to roll up a tube of paper, look through it, and trick your eye into seeing holes in people's heads. He loved that book. I still have the invisible notes he wrote in lemon juice and uncrackable codes.

Tiff took a small splash of coffee and filled the rest of her cup with milk and sugar. She contemplated sneaking Sibyl away from the table for story time in the frigid sunroom, introducing nightmares with some Little Red Riding Hood, Hansel and Gretel, Jack and the Beanstalk.

Her mother smokes, I thought, *lets the girl dress in flimsy rags in winter, and forbids the girl's father to see her. And yet it's Alice in Wonderland that'll corrupt her.* Though no one mentioned

Lenore and Doc's own saga of child endangerment running weekly in his newspaper, I longed to leap to his defense. With so few enviable qualities, our town had prided itself on its safety. You could live, as I had, from birth to old age untouched by crime—you could sleep with your doors unlocked and your windows wide open. But there's no story to be found in a town in which every hair on every head of every child is untouched.

But Doc seemed completely unbothered by Hailey's condescension. "Remember when I used to read the Miranda-and-Desiree books to you?" Doc asked Tiff. He tried to spin a teacup on his fingertip.

"Duh, of course I remember," Tiff muttered, but she didn't say, *Why would I forget that? You read to me from book three on my first night here, after Mom left.* Tiff then pulled from her back pocket a piece of paper folded into a triangle. She untucked its corners and straightened the paper against the tabletop, smoothing it out with the palms of her hands.

"Dear family," Tiff read, without any other introduction, *"I love you all very much, please always remember that. But I have something to tell you that I hope won't make you not love me. I feel a little juggled around"* (and though I think I was the only one to notice, Doc distractedly picked up a decorative clementine from the table

and jiggled it in his palm, testing its weight), *"and I would like very much to move in with Essie. I think that this is a very good decision for these reasons: (1) I need to get away from family drama; (2) Essie is getting older, and I want to spend as much time as possible with her; (3) Essie is getting older and needs help from someone younger, to open pill bottles and to help her get dressed someday when she can't dress herself right. I hope you will respect my decision. I love you. Love, Tiff."*

Ivy tried to look unrattled by plucking a cherry from the cherry-pie filling she'd used to sauce the cake, popping it into her mouth. But she chewed hard. "Did you two cook this up together?" she said. "You and your great-grandmother?"

"Of course not," I said. "This is the first I've heard of it. I don't need help with pill bottles. I don't take pills. I don't even take aspirin." It was true, this was the first I'd heard of Tiff's intentions, but I was only pretending to be offended.

"You expect me to believe that you all haven't been plotting this together?" Ivy said.

"Mom, okay, see," Tiff said, "this is exactly what I'm talking about."

"And how, exactly, is this exactly what you're talking about?" Ivy said.

"I just don't think you get to be mad about this," Tiff said.

"Tiff," Doc said, "I think maybe we should talk about this some other . . ." Hailey took a pin back from her coffee cup and appeared to push at her cuticles with it.

"I 'don't get to be mad about this,' " Ivy said. "I probably never get to be the one who gets to be mad. Right? Because I'm the terrible mother who abandoned her daughter. I'm the one who spends her life apologizing. I'm not *ever* going to be the one who gets to be mad."

"I'm sorry to interrupt," Hailey said, pushing the pin back into her chignon, "and this is going to sound like I'm leaving because of the conversation you're having, but really I'm not, we really do have to go. Speaking of pills, Sibyl has meds she has to take at a certain hour, and it is getting a little past her bedtime."

"No, no," Ivy said, standing, "please stay." She returned her attention to Tiff. "You're sick of the family drama, Tiff? You might be surprised to know that I am too. I need a few days to myself, so I hope your moving in with Granny takes effect immediately. We'll talk when we talk."

As Ivy stepped away from the table and walked through the kitchen, collecting her poncho and umbrella, Tiff called after her. *"Mom,"* she said, her pleading tone met only with the slam of the back door. Doc, meanwhile, escorted Hailey and Sibyl to the front door, apologizing to Hailey as he helped her into her coat. He then took up three clementines and did a quickie juggling act for Sibyl. After they left, Doc headed upstairs, not stomping but certainly delighting in the echoing creak of each rickety step.

"Are you mad too, Uncle Doc?" Tiff yelled, her hands cupping around her mouth like a megaphone.

"Yep," he said, though it didn't sound all that convincing.

"I should probably go talk to Mom," Tiff said.

I lowered my voice and gestured for Tiff to sit. "You don't have to be responsible for your mother's emotions," I whispered. I turned in my chair to pull a pad of paper and a pencil from a drawer of the secretary in the corner, and together Tiff and I came up with a shopping list, plotting out several menus, starting with the next morning's breakfast—a tin of blueberries for pancakes, packets of instant cocoa, and a bag of marshmallows in Christmas shapes.

· *44* ·

I called Tiff in sick to school the next morning, as we wanted to move some of her things over while Ivy was away for the day. Ivy volunteered in the town of Lemontree, having secured a place for herself on a subcommittee involved in the management of the Myrtle Kingsley Fitch home, based on Ivy's undergraduate research into the author, her own years in Paris, and a letter of recommendation she'd been carrying around for years from the professor she'd loved, written before their affair had gone sour. In the little house in Lemontree, its long lazy-Sunday porch choked by runaway bittersweet vine, Myrtle Fitch had been born. She'd later abandoned it, and later still returned to it to die.

After only a few trips back and forth between Ivy's house and mine, Tiff and I grew tired with the move and irritated with the constant drizzly sleet, so we confined ourselves to the house in our kimonos. Finally, bored by our boredom, we went to the cellar to unearth a box of baking accoutrements—the pinwheel-cookie spritzer, the candy thermometer, the snowman- and Santa-shaped cookie cutters. We successfully managed some fudge and peanut brittle, but our springerles failed to spring—they were flat where they should've been puffy, due most likely to the baker's ammonia that had sat in my pantry for ages growing impotent.

As darkness fell, guilt and anxiety nagged. We expected to hear from Ivy, and when we didn't, we weren't sure of the proper response. Would it just aggravate things to call her?

"Won't it hurt her feelings if we don't at least check on her?" Tiff asked as she stirred and stirred and stirred the pot of caramel on the stove, holding her weakening wrist with her other hand.

"I mean, the weather's nasty. Maybe the highway was slick. Shouldn't we call and make sure she got home okay?"

Ivy's not calling, not stopping by, whether calculated or not, had very effectively dropped Tiff into a funk, summoning up all those years of Ivy's indifference. We rushed the caramel just a bit, intending to put on our coats and carry a plate of peacemaking cookies to Ivy's. Before we could embark on our sisterly gesture of goodwill, however, the doorbell rang.

Tiff and I peeped around the front parlor's drapes. The thin old man at the door might easily have been mistaken for an exorcist, with his long black trench coat and black hat, his black pants and black galoshes, were it not for the bright red umbrella, its price tag dangling from one of the ribs and whipping in the wind. He stood hunched, his one hand clutching the lapel of his coat closed at his throat.

The bell rang again, a grating and unmelodic buzz I would've replaced years before had it not been so infrequently used. Tiff and I went to the door, both still in our coats over our kimonos. "Yes?" I said to the man.

"You don't recognize me," the man said.

"Oh, my sweet Lord," Tiff said. The author photo on the backs of all his books was from his earliest days as a writer, decades before, but Tiff nonetheless identified him. In the photo he sits slump-shouldered, captured in the middle of a lunge for the typewriter like the Phantom of the Opera about to pound out a melody, his hair undone from its waxy pompadour, his fingers hovering bent above the keys.

Part

· 45 ·

In the foyer, I took Muscatine's coat and hat. "This garish umbrella was the best I could do in the airport gift shop," he said. "Everything was red-and-white football regalia." Tiff only stared at him, and she seemed to shrink in age before my very eyes, freckling, her wide eyes consuming her face. Muscatine quickly played into it. He leaned forward, gnarling his bony hands into claws, his horror-show shadow stretching along the wall. "My hunger is trying to gnaw its way out of my gut," he told her. "Let's satisfy it before it rips its way through." Tiff appeared to be stifling a genuine scream.

Part of me felt compelled to scream as well. As thrilled as I was, I was a little terrified too. When the letters had been simply bits of wonder that flitted in and out of my often-empty mailbox, it had been easy to keep it all hush-hush—it had seemed a romantic fantasy. I glanced across the street as I closed the front door, eyeballing all of Doc's lit windows for any sign of him catching sight of my guest. Doc wouldn't understand my wanting to keep my correspondence secret. I now saw my actions as Doc might: they seemed a betrayal. *He* would never keep anything like this from *me*.

"Tiff," I said, "go clear off the dining room

table, and I'll throw something together for Mr. Muscatine." After dragging over boxes of Tiff's things that morning, we'd only managed to abandon them in the dining room, on the table of cherrywood that seated twelve but had years before become the house's catchall. On one end was a jigsaw puzzle of a swarm of midnight-blue butterflies that I'd long since dismissed as unfinishable. Stacked on a few of the chairs were *New Yorker*s I'd never gotten around to reading but intended to donate to the nursing home. A few tin boxes of recipe cards, some accordion files of government papers, a basket of reading glasses I've collected over the years. Even if you overlooked all that old-lady clutter, when you turned on the overhead light, you could smell the dust on the burning bulbs of the chandelier, that hot tickle in your nose that threatens a sneeze.

"Thank you," he said. "Meanwhile, I'll sit in this here seat"—pointing to the chair with the embroidered cushion—"and wrestle off these rain boots."

Tiff and I tossed off our own coats and rushed about the kitchen and dining room. That morning, we'd bought a box of frozen French fries, which I sprinkled across a cookie tin with some sea salt, and I took a bucket of leftover beef stew from my freezer. As I prepared the impromptu dinner, I heard Muscatine chatting with Tiff about his fear of flying.

Bent at the back by its weight, I carried my silver coffee set to the table, inching forward like a chambermaid straight out of Poe. I then returned to the kitchen for the bowl of stew and plate of fries for Muscatine.

Whenever you want to know something significant about someone, you must watch them eat. If you marry a girl who talks as she chews, that talking-as-she's-chewing, three squares a day, may be grounds for divorce. A man who can't let his peas touch his gravy, or a woman who can't keep her fork from scratching against her teeth—it may all seem small, and may reveal nothing about true character, but we eat too often with each other to pretend that our dining habits don't matter greatly.

Which is to say, Muscatine ate like no one I'd like to eat with regularly. All his complaint about hunger pains, about how he couldn't stomach eating before or during a flight, all my scurrying about the kitchen looking for quick fixings, and he only nibbled and pecked. He even commented on the heavy weight of the utensils.

But it wasn't just his bird-like picking at my stew that seemed to indicate ingratitude. I found myself somehow reading his disappointment in practically his every aspect, even in the way the press of his hat had left a red line on his bald head and the way his ears still glowed pink from the wind; how a stitch on his necktie had snagged loose and his watch slipped around on his wrist. He should be enraptured every second of his life, it seemed to me. After all, he could go anywhere, do anything.

I considered myself much too old for disappointment—I'd long ago gotten used to the notion of not living different lives. That I was stuck with the life I've lived was a conclusion I'd come to a lifetime ago. But to have had his opportunities of adventure, of transformation—I nearly could not forgive him. How could he entertain even a moment of being dissatisfied with anything at all? But I'd egged him on in our letters. Had he not felt I would lovingly indulge him, he would never have confided in me.

"Do you have any children of your own, Mr. Muscatine?" Tiff asked.

"I did," he said. As he spoke, he leaned over and picked up a piece of the jigsaw puzzle and almost instantly identified its place. He then did so with another piece of the puzzle, and another. "I do. Well, I have the daughter of the wife I used to have." He took a deep breath, then reached across to pick up my coffee cup. He swirled the dregs around like a reader of tea leaves, plucked a pair of bifocals from the basket on the chair, and held them before his eyes.

"What do you see?" I said.

"The Crippled Eighty," he said.

· 46 ·

While we'd been feeding Muscatine, Daisy had returned to the CB. Whenever she read from this alternative version of *Coffins*, her mood would lighten enough to keep her awake the rest of the night, imagining Lenore upstairs, safe in her bed and drifting into a dream. The evening's bedtime story would shape the world of Lenore's sleep, and Lenore would be among the girls of Rothgutt's in a long cotton nightgown with a candle in hand, spiders and bats creeping the dream into nightmare.

After reading, Daisy always felt physically lighter, and she had taken to closing all the curtains tight with clothespins before dancing an uninspired ballet. She spun around the front room, avoiding furniture, faking pirouettes, sweeping out her arms and twisting her wrists, turning in circles on the balls of her bare feet. She even curtsied for her audience of no one, pinching the bottom of her daisy-print dress and lifting it only slightly as she bent her knees.

"Stop acting like a little girl," her father had told her whenever she'd pretended to be a ballerina. *But am I not,* she had wondered, *a little girl?* He mocked all her childhood distractions and dreaminess, so she read books only in the bathtub where he wouldn't come in and sneer at her. He

223

dismissed everything she read as "smutty romance," though she'd never read romance and for the longest time didn't know what *smutty* meant. She even adopted the word into her own vocabulary incorrectly, thinking smut was what made your fingertips gray when the pages got wet with bathwater. When she ate toast and jam, she'd say she needed a napkin for her smutty fingers; when she got the bottom of her feet dirty, she needed to hose them off to clean up the smut. No one ever corrected her, and soon enough even her mother and father took to using the word in Daisy's way.

But the books Daisy used to read had been Daisy's mother's. Daisy would sneak the books from the boxes pushed beneath her mother's tall bed; she'd reach in indiscriminately and read whatever she pulled out. Her mother had gone to college with intentions of becoming an English teacher, but she'd met Daisy's father at a football game, where he'd shared with her the spiced rum in his thermos. He'd proposed three months later, and because he'd been on such exceptional behavior, she'd accepted his proposal, not knowing she didn't know him at all. She'd thought him a handsome dummy with a wicked sense of humor, a vast improvement on all the unfunny college boys she'd seemed to attract. She hadn't hated how rough he'd been on her wedding night—she'd liked it, somewhat, the firm hand, the harsh voice, which had all spoken to her own history with a cold and commanding father—but the night had changed her by morning. She'd gone from a college girl settling for less than she deserved to a bit of a tragic heroine.

The Crippled Eighty had been a kind of salvation for Daisy's mother. She had slipped effortlessly into her role as matriarch of the homestead and had often spent the whole day in her housecoat. She'd had a colorful collection of silken robes sent in the mail from her old college roommate, who'd married better and traveled the world.

Daisy's mother had been the one to dub the farm the Crippled Eighty, certain its lack of flatness, its roll of short hills, would ruin irrigation and any shots at a crop, but it had pleased her to be wrong. She'd grown to love the farm and its lush acres of green in the summer.

"Promise me," Daisy's mother had told Daisy one summer afternoon as they'd sunned themselves on beach towels that had come free with boxes of detergent, "that even after you've outgrown your father and me—which you will—that you never turn your back on the Crippled Eighty." Calling the farm by name had seemed to Daisy's mother highly civilized, lending dignity to what, to others, might only be agriculture. As they lay back in their swimsuits and floppy hats, they drank root-beer floats and shooed mosquitoes from their skin. "This farm can be a kind of security for you, which is something I never had. Keep one foot on it always. You'll want somewhere to run back to sometimes."

For the longest time, Daisy thought her mother was referring to the farm as the Crippled *Lady,* and she'd imagined the land as a nude woman reclining. This crippled lady, lying prone, seemed powerful and majestic. It reminded Daisy of the joke she'd read, and had never understood, in *The Book of Sick Jokes* (bought at the drugstore), which had stayed in her consciousness, picking at her with its mystery, for years: *She's so fat that when she lies around the house, she lies* around *the house.* The joke had had no meaning to Daisy beyond her perception of the Crippled Lady, ruined by weight, surrounding everything like God.

· *47* ·

S he's doing some kind of dance," Muscatine said. He looked through the window of the front door, peeking through the holes in the leaves of the roses in the lace curtain.

"Dancing?" I said. Tiff and I had helped him onto the property by lifting the slat of the fence for him to wriggle through. Muscatine's scarf had snagged on the thorns of a bush, and I noticed he now bled from a scratch on the side of his neck.

Tiff and I too looked through the window and saw that, indeed, Daisy was dancing. It seemed I'd seen Daisy in all sorts of states of chaos and breakdown—I'd seen Daisy drop into muteness, and I'd seen her flap her gums too much. I'd seen Daisy morose, excited. Hopeful, despairing. But this clumsy dance, it was a new ripple. I squinted, cringing, as I wanted to see and not see at the same time. Had Muscatine not been standing there, I might have stood watching until her room went dark.

Finally I knocked. "It's S Myles," I said loudly through the door. The rush of shadows against the curtains stilled, and what seemed several seconds later, Daisy opened the door. Strands of her hair stuck to the sweat of her forehead and cheeks. "This is Wilton Muscatine, Daisy," I said.

Daisy, seemingly unsurprised and not at all starstruck, reached toward Muscatine's head. He flinched, leaning back in his galoshes, but she continued reaching forward to touch him, to bring back a few fingers with spots of blood. She held them up for him to see. "You're bleeding," she said. "We'll fix it." She gestured us in and with the brusque competence of a farmwife, led us to the kitchen, where she lifted a teakettle from the stove and put it in the sink. "Make some tea for us," she told me. "I'll tend to his cut."

Tiff kept to the shadows of the hallway, not wanting Daisy to recognize her from before, when the kitchen had been thick with Lenorians, back when she'd stormed in with that plank. But Tiff was difficult not to notice in her kimono and parka and the cowboy boots she'd pulled on in her rush out the front door—black leather boots stamped with red hearts. As she'd stepped from my pickup truck, she'd worried about her white-blond hair, even with the dark roots now spidering out from her scalp. Daisy, she knew, had objected to children in her company, especially girls with hair the color of corn silk. Behind the seat I'd had only one hat, a broad-brimmed straw hat I gardened in, and she'd tucked her hair up into it and pulled on the bead of the neck strap to tighten it under her chin.

As I filled the kettle, I looked around the kitchen at things that had not been there before. Now, in the absence of Lenore, were sudden signs of children—pinned to the fridge with magnets were finger paintings and macaroni art. Propped up in a chair in the corner was a teddy bear in a fancy bonnet.

Daisy returned to the kitchen table to dab at Muscatine's neck with a washcloth, and she applied a bandage patterned with cartoon unicorns. I brought the mismatched mugs of tea— bags of honey-mint was all I'd found in the pantry—to the table, then attended to some cleaning, wiping down the countertops, putting dishes away. I plucked a wooden spoon from where it soaked in a bowl of water in the sink. I resisted telling Daisy she shouldn't soak her wooden spoons lest they crack.

"When Lenore was here, we had Miranda-and-Desiree Band-Aids, actually," Daisy said. She described the bandages and how they'd been decorated with illustrations of the banged-up faces of the girls of Rothgutt's. Miranda had had a black eye and a swollen lip. Desiree had had a seeping gash on her forehead and a red nose all out of joint.

"I can't imagine the scratch is as much as you're making it out to be," Muscatine said.

"Lenore would never forgive me if I didn't look after you," Daisy said.

"Lenore," Muscatine said, mumbling, musing, already picking at the edge of the Band-Aid on his neck. "Can I see where Lenore slept?" he said.

As we followed Daisy and Muscatine up the stairs, Tiff took my arm in hers, and we leaned in toward each other like sisters lost. "Why did Muscatine come to see you?" Tiff whispered in my ear.

"He knows me by my obituaries," I whispered back.

Whereas Lenore's room had once been spare and empty, devoid of any girlish concerns, it had since become overrun with childhood. Atop the bed's ruffled pink quilt was a small menagerie of stuffed animals. A paper lantern, powered by a motor with a soothing hum, spun slowly atop the nightstand, sending silhouettes of fish and mermaids swimming along the wall. And stuck in the corners of the vanity mirror were photo after photo of children posing for their school portraits, their smiles caged by orthodontia, their pigtails drawn what looked to be painfully tight, or their collars or pinafores freshly stiffened.

"Some of these children are missing," Daisy said, running her fingers along the edge of the vanity mirror. "Some of them aren't. People send them to me from all over, to comfort me. I don't know how people think I could be comforted by the missing." She sat on the little stool in front of the mirror, folding her hands in her lap. She took a breath, and as she exhaled, her posture slackened. She seemed tired of us, all of us. She seemed the Little Match Girl in reverse, escaping into not a happy fantasy but a darker one, into deeper delusions of loss.

Muscatine, perhaps seizing on this vulnerability, stood behind Daisy and buttoned the top buttons at the back of her dress, the ones she must've been unable to reach. "Can I see the book?" he said.

"What book?" Daisy said.

"The book you've been reading from," he said. "The one Lenore wrote. I'd just like to look at it."

Daisy stayed seated. "During the last big storm,

when the power went out, Lenore read by candlelight," she said. She picked up a plastic bottle of a girl's nail glitter and brushed some onto her thumbnail. "She wanted to hurry and finish the tenth Miranda-and-Desiree before summer ended. Not even the noise of the wind tearing everything up outside could stop her." I could see Lenore as we'd been seeing all our children that summer and fall—her longing for the final book even as she dreaded the story ending forever. Maybe that was what made us so vulnerable to the mythology of Lenore—the fragility of childhood, and the heartbreak of it, and how, when you're so young, a season can seem endless.

Daisy put the nail polish away, stood, and left the room, crooking her finger, beckoning us to follow her. Muscatine touched one of the photos on the vanity. He seemed to be considering filching it, but he snapped his hand away quickly when Daisy poked her head back in. "Come with me," she said. She led us downstairs to where her CB sat atop a sideboard of dark wood. She opened the top drawer and took from it the red notebook, which she handed to Muscatine. He opened the notebook with reverence.

"Logophilia," he muttered. Tiff and I later looked it up, a magnifying glass hovering over the minuscule print of my dictionary that had warped with the weight of its own sodden, stained pages, our eyes watering from the dust—*logophilia: an obsession with words.* "I'd like to buy this from you," he said. He took from his coat pocket a handful of wadded-up cash, as if children had paid him directly with their sweaty clutches of dollar bills.

· *48* ·

Daisy invited us to leave. We all three slunk from the house, mortified, bundled up in our coats not so much from the cold as from embarrassment, and we barely spoke as Tiff chauffeured us back toward town. Muscatine offered me a black licorice cough drop from his coat pocket, and I refused with a curt shake of my head.

"Are you mad at me?" he asked.

"No," I lied. "I just don't happen to have a cough."

"But you eat cough drops all the time, you said. Even when you don't cough."

I didn't remember having mentioned that in my letters to him. Had I really revealed something so mundane? But it pleased me that he remembered, and he seemed pleased that I was pleased, so I politely took the cough drop from him, exchanging a static shock with the touch of our fingertips. We both took responsibility for the static, and we both apologized, but we said nothing more until we pulled up in front of the bed-and-breakfast where

Muscatine was booked under an assumed name. Trammell House was a little seafoam-green Victorian with plastic sunflower-shaped pinwheels spinning unseasonably among the bare rosebushes.

"We don't smoke in Trammell House," he said, feigning snootiness, eyebrow raised, digging for his cigarettes. "But these old houses are full of poison. They're killing their guests with mold and radon and gas leaks. At least my cigarette has a filter to protect me." He kept still, the unlit cigarette between his fingers. "Hey," he said, his mood suddenly lifting, "you should come in for a drink! Mrs. Trammell said to help myself to anything in the credenza."

Tiff said, "I don't touch the stuff," which made Muscatine giggle. He still didn't move from the pickup.

"I just wanted to read the book, that's all," he said after a pause. "I didn't mean to upset her."

"Give me a spoiler," Tiff said. "From the real book. Yours. Do they find their mother?"

"They're sent home to their mother, but they don't much care for her. So they join a traveling carnival, feigning a conjoined life." I'm not sure that Tiff believed him—it sounded like a destiny Muscatine invented on the spot. Sensing her doubt, he continued, "They spend the rest of their days and nights, onstage and off, wearing one dress made from two dresses sewn together." He checked Tiff's reaction again, then ventured forth with more: "They see all the world—Paris, Morocco, the North and South Poles." He paused. "They wear shared bloomers." He paused again. "They change their names to Sherry and Cheri, the Von Splitt Twins."

"I love it!" Tiff said, probably just to get him to stop.

We said our good-nights, and we promised we'd write.

"Be good to your granny," Muscatine told Tiff. "And to your mother. Kindness to your family costs you almost nothing but affords a wealth of goodwill."

"Is that from something?" I asked. "Did somebody say that?"

"Not that I know of," he said. "I guess *I* said it. Just now."

I put my hand on his arm. "Don't worry too much about your daughter," I said.

He patted my hand and shrugged. "The son of A. A. Milne—the inspiration for Christopher Robin—died furious at his father," he said. "He accused his father of blemishing his good name. And the little boy named Peter who inspired J. M. Barrie to create Peter Pan? He eventually committed suicide. And so did the son of Kenneth Grahame, the author of *The Wind in the Willows*. Tossed themselves under a train, both of them. Well, different trains, at different times."

As he stepped from the pickup, he said,

seemingly as an afterthought, "I want you to write my obituary, as a matter of fact."

"I'll die long before you do," I said. "How old are you, anyway?"

"I'm sixty-eight," he said.

"A baby," I said. His gaze had been often defined as child-like, probably because of its pristine glassiness. His eyes looked as if freshly bought from an oculist's cabinet.

"I'll commission you to write my obit now," he said, "while we're both alive; then we'll auction it off for some charity. We'll save lives with my obituary. What a way to go, ay?"

I watched him as he returned to Trammell House, as he followed every exaggerated curve in the winding stone walk. Only as he attempted to spark his cigarette with a lighter in the sleet did we all realize he'd left his umbrella in the umbrella-shaped umbrella stand in my front hallway.

· 49 ·

Tiff and I stayed up late drinking cocoa in the parlor, Tiff on the sofa with Muscatine's red umbrella opened above her, its handle against her shoulder as she spun it around like a parasol. She parted the sheers of the front window with her pinkie and glanced across the street. "It's really kind of obvious, don't you think?" she said. "I move in with my mom, and days later, Doc's got another family in the works."

"I'm not sure that's what's happening," I said.

"I just think he needs to be careful with those two. In case you haven't noticed, they're a real couple of weaklings. If he gets that little girl attached to him, it's going to tear her up when things don't work out with Hailey."

"Things aren't going to work out with Hailey?" I said.

Tiff shrugged and fell contemplative. "I think the reason I'm an insomniac," she said, "is because I was born at midnight. Don't you think it's terrible that doctors spank babies first thing? An act of abuse right from the get-go."

"I don't know if they do that anymore," I said.

"Why did they ever do it to begin with?"

"I don't know," I said. "Maybe you can tell if the baby's breathing properly if it shrieks like a banshee."

"You had a baby once," Tiff said. "It didn't occur to you to ask them why they were beating the hell out of your newborn?"

"I was probably feeling a little beaten down myself at the moment," I said. Just before my son's birth, we'd moved to a tiny town in a valley of the sandhills of western Nebraska, where my husband had had ambitions of becoming a cattle rancher. I would spend my days pregnant and eating peanuts by the handful, my typewriter balanced precipitously on a deep windowsill in the bunkhouse, writing my obituaries and letting the peanut shells just fall on the floor. My father would mail me news of the latest dead, and I'd mail back to him the obits I wrote. The typewriter had been pushed up against a crack in the glass of the window that had been just wide enough for a rattler to slither through one afternoon as I wrote about the dearly departed Cloris Thorne, who'd drowned in a flooded ravine. A neighbor came over to club the snake with the back of his hoe.

"What time of day was my mom born?" Tiff asked. "What was that day like?"

"I actually don't really recall," I said. "I think I remember her father handing out bubble-gum cigars to the nurses. But maybe that was when Doc was born."

"What time of day was Doc born?"

I shook my head and sighed. "I don't recall that either." I saw a gnat on the brim of my cup. It struggled in a bubble of my hot cocoa gone cold, and I wiped it away with my thumb.

"Did you write any of it down in a baby book? Did you write it down anywhere?" Tiff asked.

"No," I said. "If I did, I don't know where it would be."

"Now that's all just lost?" Tiff said, clucking her tongue. "It's all just gone, that family history? Why wouldn't you at least write it down?"

"Who thinks they'll ever forget?" I said. "And who thought my son would die before I did?"

I told Tiff about my house in the sandhills, the rattler, and how, after the rattler had nearly fanged me, my father had written a stern letter to my husband, threatening to come up and collect me himself if he didn't abandon his ranching career and bring me home straightaway to have my baby in a civilized manner, in a land where the snakes were of a toothless variety.

Tiff pulled from her pocket her cell phone and began to text herself. "I'm writing that down," she said. "*Rattler. Sandhills.* You don't get to just take our whole family history with you, S."

Tiff appeared to feel bad for evoking the very real possibility of my imminent death, and she returned her gaze back across the street, to Doc's dark house. When I heard a few sniffles, I asked her if she was crying behind the umbrella, and she said no.

It's startling, Ivy had said to Tiff the other day, in relation to some mouthy comment Tiff had tossed off in my direction, *the way you talk to your great-grandma. You're too familiar with her.*

Yes, she's familiar with me, I'd snapped at Ivy, right there in front of Tiff, *because I've been there for her for years.* I'd immediately felt guilty for saying it, but she simply hadn't understood what damage she might be doing. If Tiff became angry with me, felt the need to tiptoe, what would become of all that we had?

"Somebody's here again," Tiff mumbled, her jaw resting on the back of the sofa. "A guy on a bike."

I answered the door when the young man knocked, and he handed me a brown-paper bag stapled shut, with an envelope attached. "An old guy at my mom's B-and-B gave me a hundred bucks to drop this by," he said, grinning, seeming to be under the impression he'd suckered someone.

Back in the parlor, Tiff tore into the sack to discover that Muscatine had sneaked her a copy of *The Coffins of Little Hope*, and without a word, she ran her fingers along the grooves of the embossed letters of the title. I opened the envelope. *You'll see that I lied,* Muscatine wrote, *when you asked me to spoil the plot.*

Despite my constant criticizing her for it, Tiff had always been one of those children who read the last page first of every book. The pages of *Coffins*, made from pulverized coffee chaff and dryer lint and other charming refuse, were peppered with wildflower seeds. Tiff lay on her back in front of the fireplace and read aloud to me the last paragraph, the narrator directing his reader to rip the pages out and bury them in the dirt of the yard or, for the unfortunate urbanites, in the narrow soil of a window box. *If the flowers struggle up, strangling from the dirt, then bloom in the sun,* the narrator says in the final lines of the final chapter of this final book, *you'll know that Miranda and Desiree finally escaped the walls of Rothgutt's, and they've been to spy in your windows, to laugh and weep at the lovely life you lead, to be jealous of even your worst circumstances. As they've mocked you for not appreciating all the wonderful things you have, seeds have spilled from the holes in their apron pockets. But even if no flowers grow, please don't worry. We're sure Miranda and Desiree are fine, nonetheless. Quite sure of it. Please, please, we beg that you don't worry at all. Don't give yourself a stomachache about it, for God's sake. They're very, very, very, very resourceful girls, as I'm sure you've come to realize. They'll be just fine, I suppose.*

Tiff flipped back to the front of the book. Only a few chapters in, after I'd nodded off several times as she read to me, I felt my head fall back and my eyes close, but I seemed somehow to be reading the page, the story taking an even more fantastical slant—babies plucked the wings off frogs—and then I was reading about *myself* at Rothgutt's, an orphaned girl, having been locked away for having killed her own mother in childbirth. I was thirteen, but in that way of dreams, I was also an old woman, and in a blink the mother I'd killed became Lenore in a glass coffin. In her breath that fogged the glass, Lenore wrote, *Wake up*. I looked around at the other girls to see if they saw what I saw, and when I tried to speak, to tell them Lenore was alive, I couldn't find the right words.

I woke up then, saying, "Wake up," and Tiff laughed at me.

"Go to bed," she said, and her eyes fell back upon the page. She put her finger to the paper, just beneath the words, to guide herself along; so densely packed were the narrow lines of text that she often accidentally reread the line she'd just finished reading, as if the book conspired to keep her stuck, sending the same images through her thoughts in a loop.

· 50 ·

I woke in my bed late in the morning, though I couldn't remember having left the parlor. I sat up and called out Tiff's name, hoping she wouldn't answer, hoping she'd had the sense to go to school without prompting. If I let her stay home a second day in a row, I feared there'd likely be some kind of intervention. I would appear indulgent and slovenly. "Tiff!" I called again, and I heard her feet fast on the stairs.

"What is it!" she said, running up to the footboard. "Are you okay?"

"Am I okay?" I said. "No. No, not at all. I'm not

okay. I'm in deep trouble. It's ten in the morning and you're not in school, are you?"

"Don't scare me like that, Essie," she said.

"You *should* be scared," I said.

Tiff crawled into bed with me, beneath my quilts. "I haven't slept a wink," she said, smiling and fluttering her eyelashes. "I finished the book. Did you hear me fall around 2 in the morning? I had to go to the bathroom but didn't want to stop reading, and I fell *up* the stairs. I wasn't watching where I was going." She tossed the quilts aside and lifted her kimono above her knee to show me a nasty patch of black and blue on the back of her leg.

"Oh, Tiffany," I said. I went to my vanity in an effort to wrestle my hair into something presentable. "Go get dressed. I'm giving you back to your mother."

Tiff ignored me, preoccupied as she was by invading my privacy, riffling through the drawer of my nightstand. She pinched the bulb of a perfume atomizer to douse her neck and chest with a lavender scent. She slipped on my black sleeping mask, which I hadn't worn since a bout of sleeplessness in the 1950s. "Turns out that *Coffin* is the family name," Tiff said, her eyes hidden by the mask. "Miranda and Desiree Coffin. Their family lives in a village called Little Hope, which is a tiny community just outside the town of Big Hope." She shrugged, unimpressed with

Muscatine's wordplay. In Daisy's version, the coffins of the title had been means of escape, Miranda and Desiree tucked into a pair of pine boxes and liberated from the asylum in a horse-drawn hearse by a sympathetic undertaker's apprentice.

Tiff took off the mask and pinned to her sleeve a paper corsage, a true relic, from my first dance. I'd thought I'd lost it the night I'd first worn it, when some other girls and I, and some boys, had sneaked into a cornfield next to the dance hall to get liquored up. I'd returned to the field the next morning to find the corsage caught, abloom, in the crook of a stalk.

After stepping from the closet in a dress I pulled on, I sat on the edge of the bed and unpinned the flower from Tiff's sleeve. I placed it atop my nightstand and turned my back to Tiff to indicate she should zip me up.

"I'm not going anywhere with you," Tiff said, zipping.

"Don't you want to be the better person?"

"No," Tiff said. "What good would that do me?"

"Well, you *are* the better person, whether you like it or not. I've raised you right." I turned to face her, to take her hands in mine. "Your mother needs you maybe a little more than you need her. We have to be protective of her. Now, get dressed. I'm abandoning you." I returned to the vanity to situate my dragonfly hairpin.

"I like it here. You don't make me sleep, and you don't make me go to school." I caught Tiff's reflection as she stretched out in the bed, and she seemed to age a year or two in the murk of my unpolished mirror, her gangly limbs and laziness suggesting the young lady she'd be much too soon.

"You have to turn out better than all the rest of us, Tiffany," I said. "How can I die happy if you're just going to let everything fall apart?"

"Don't be morbid," she said.

I returned to the nightstand for the paper corsage and pinned it to the front of my dress. "I'm not morbid," I said, offended, touching at the delicate curl of the edge of the faded rose petal, causing the thinnest vein of a crack. "I'm *not*."

· 51 ·

Myrtle Kingsley Fitch's home had been obsessively preserved in its original state of bad housekeeping. Myrtle had spent the last two years of her early death (at fifty-four) in her childhood home, attempting to finish her unfinished novel in an upstairs study. Upon her death, a group of historians had bought the house with intentions of keeping it untouched. You should walk in and feel that she'd just stepped out, they'd reasoned. It was as if they'd longed to expose her as human; they'd even left her underthings drying on the shower rod and a half-finished bottle of wine, shut up with a broken cork, on a windowsill.

Tiff and I found Ivy in the kitchen of the Fitch House sitting on a stool and dabbing at her fingernails with a cotton ball soaked in polish remover. On a shelf above her head were jars of pickled cantaloupe that had been canned decades before. "Essie," Tiff said to me, "could you please leave me to speak to my mother alone?" just as we'd rehearsed on the hour's drive to Lemontree. Ivy seemed eased by my exclusion.

I left the kitchen and went up to the room in which Myrtle Kingsley Fitch had famously failed to write her long-awaited book. I unhooked the velvet rope, violating the historic space, and I could feel the dull thud of her writer's block, like a swelling of the sinuses. Her soul surely remained in the room, frustrated, unable to type with her weightless fingers, to finish the sentence still only partly written on the paper still partly rolled on the cylinder, all exactly as it had been on the last day of her life, when she'd simply expired from unexplained illness.

She'd written to her sister that every word was impossible. She'd said she felt she had to invent the word before she could write it down, right down to the very shapes of the letters.

Muscatine would envy Myrtle Fitch, sapped and tongue-tied. He had written to me once of his desire to never write again. If only he could look at a naked page and see nothing but the grain of the paper and its flecks of pulp, he'd told me. Then, perhaps, he could begin to fathom the simplicities of existence—he could just do what everyone else did; he could fall in love, then out of love, then into love with someone else. If he didn't write, he was certain, he could concentrate on his own well-being. But when he looked at a sheet of paper, it was as if the words were already written there—he just had to slip his pen into the groove of the cursive.

· 52 ·

When I returned to my house alone that afternoon, it appeared as if someone had broken in and lived there for days, quite comfortably, in my few hours of absence. My dining room had been straightened in a messy manner, the kitchen sink stacked with soiled dishes and pans, the stovetop spattered with chocolate and burned sugar, all just as we'd left it. Even Muscatine's red umbrella sat open on the floor of the parlor, begging for bad luck. Tiff had been with me not even two days, yet I felt her absence so severely, I was winded by it, my legs trembling, my breaths cut short. I dropped into the dining room chair in which Muscatine had sat, and I wept, not at all gently. I sobbed for a full minute or two, giving myself hiccups, happy to have all the noise.

In an effort to ease the hiccups, I picked up Muscatine's coffee cup and swallowed the dregs, my lips where his lips had been. I unpinned my paper corsage and attempted to repair a loose petal, tucking it in deeper among the other paper petals. And after making the repair, I began to tear at it. The delicate thing had implausibly survived decades. Touching its dusty folds, hearing its crinkling between my fingers, always brought back that evening of the dance, the laughter in the field, our dresses lit silver by the half of a moon. In my tipsiness, two boys stole quick and innocent kisses, and one of the girls stole one from me too, and my voice turned so raspy and scratched from the booze that I sang the hymns I knew by heart just to hear the low and broken notes. My sister had always been the pretty one, I the homely one, but for this one evening, I felt transformed.

For so many years I'd remembered every minute of that evening, the drive to the dance, the dance itself, our stumbling deeper and deeper into the fields to disappear from the reach of the light of the Chinese lanterns.

Soon enough, I suppose, I'll only remember having once remembered it.

The paper rose, in its plucked and pulverized state on my table, would now remind me not of the dance of my youth but rather of this fit of my old age.

Instead of tidying the house, I put together a plate of cookies and candy, put on my fur, walked across the street, and let myself in through Doc's kitchen door. I hung my coat on a closet doorknob and began to clean *his* kitchen, though it didn't much need it. I sprinkled some bleach in the sink and started to scrub. I heard Doc calling to me from another room.

"Oh!" I called back. "You scared me half to death. I thought I was alone."

"Nope," Doc said. "Not alone."

I peeked around the corner to where Doc sat at the end of the dining room table. Spread out before him were various tricks and novelties he'd collected over the years—the Chinese finger cuffs and thumb guillotines, a top hat, a magic wand, a birdcage with a trapdoor, a knotted scarf tangled up in interlocking gold rings. I sat at the end of the table and folded my hands; I still wore the rubber gloves from the sink.

"I thought you'd be at work," I said.

"Actually," he said, "I kind of need to talk to you about that."

"Are you throwing out your toys?" I said.

He slipped his hand into a puppet—a white rabbit—and performed some inexpert ventriloquism, muttering out the side of his mouth in a gangster squeal, "Who you calling a 'toy,' lady?"

We all kept silent, even the rabbit.

I removed my gloves. "Is it too early for a glass of wine?"

"Yes," Doc said as he stood and walked to the sideboard to pour us each a glass from a half-empty bottle, a white zinfandel from a young vineyard in central Nebraska, a wine that tasted like flat soda pop, sweet and thick enough to soak your pancakes with. Doc came to my end of the table to sit and drink with me.

"Since there's no easy way to tell you this, I'll just tell you the truth straight out. I've been thinking a lot about closing down the County Paragraph," he said.

"Well," I said, "maybe you should stop thinking a lot about it." In only fifteen more years, the County Paragraph would celebrate its centennial—one hundred years of continuous publication, every drop of ink overseen by the men in my family.

"When I said I should tell you the truth, I meant to say, I should tell you the actual truth, and the truth is . . ." He stopped to take a drink of wine, and I did too. "The truth is that I'm closing down the County Paragraph. And I hope to sell the printing press."

"You need to sell the newspaper too," I said.

"Who would buy it?"

"Subscriptions are up," I said.

"They went back down," he said.

"Wilton Muscatine subscribes," I said. "I know because he writes me letters." I then confessed everything—Muscatine's abbreviated correspondence dashed off on scraps of paper, his shocking arrival in our town, his offer to buy the red notebook from Daisy. I had Doc's interest, I knew it. As he bit at his lip and ran his finger along the stem of his glass, I could see him already retelling, in his mind, the story to others, framing the details.

But then, as if he thought I'd slipped into senile nattering, he took my hand and smiled pathetically. "I have to do this," he said. He'd been talking to Hailey, he explained. Together they'd fantasized about the very thing he'd dreaded for so long—our town square transformed into a tourist trap, a candy-colored replica of what it had once been. The newspaper office could become a shop of books and novelties. He could sell that wretchedly sweet wine, and pipe tobacco, and peppermint sticks from apothecary jars. Hailey knew of grants intended to rescue little choking towns.

"I'll write about the Muscatine letters," I said. "For the newspaper. I'll write about everything he told me. They're very revealing. They're historic." I don't know if I would've made such a morally corrupt suggestion had I not felt I'd been slightly abandoned by Muscatine. His visit had been, somehow, an act of retreat. He'd come to our town hoping his fame would allow him to collect something of ours—he'd hoped to snatch out from under us the red notebook. And I suspected his letters to me would now end.

"I don't think you're hearing me, Essie," Doc said, and with that I burst into tears for the second time that afternoon.

I then violated my own principles and sought to punish in the same cruel fashion that other old ladies punished *their* families. I held my hand to my face. "Couldn't you have waited until I was dead?" I said above my sobbing. And Doc punished me right back by saying nothing, by not touching my back or my wrist, not attempting to comfort me at all. He was right to ignore me. We'd been through too much, knew each other too well, to resort to such pedestrian methods of guilt.

"Anyway, you can't," I said. "You can't shut the paper down. It doesn't belong to you. It's not a matter of ownership, it's a matter of responsibility. You have a responsibility. This town has given us their trust. You can't be callous with it."

"I'm not callous," he said.

"Not callous!" I stood from the table with my glass of wine and walked to the sideboard to refill it, though I'd had only a sip or two. "You're going to put a candy store in the newspaper offices?"

"Actually," he said, enthusiastic, "there's going to be a storefront like the one your dad had in the earliest days of the paper. I'm going to put up some of the old tin advertising we've been keeping in the basement. I'll wear an apron and sell fancy coffee. I'll do magic tricks. I'll be the town eccentric. We'll probably make a fortune in cigar sales alone."

"Not even a sports page?" I said. "Your kid joins the Little League and there's no picture of the team to clip out and put on your refrigerator? How does a town even know what it is, or who's in it, if there's no newspaper? Things happen and they just turn to ether?"

"There's still a newspaper in Bonnevilla," he said. "I just spoke to the editor today. Anything worth covering here, it'll cover."

I looked down at the bottle of wine and knocked my knuckles against the top of the sideboard. "But don't you see? It's not about what's *worth* covering. What about all the things that aren't worth anything to anyone but us?" I was feeling, in that moment, that I'd outlived everything worthwhile in my life.

Doc stepped up to me and put his hand on my back. He spoke close to my good ear. "I'm thirty-eight years old, and I'm exhausted, Grandma," he said. "I've spent most of my life being a sixty-year-old man. I can't be an old man anymore. I may be making a terrible mistake, but even if I am, it can't be worse than where I am now. Having my every word read and scrutinized and condemned by any hick with fifty cents? This is not . . . *dignity* that I have. My God, how many nights have I sat up awake, hoping for the worst for Daisy? I've been desperate for the worst possible conclusion. What, I wanted Lenore to exist so that she could be held captive somewhere? Or I wanted Daisy to confess so we'd all know she was insane? Wouldn't it have been better to have left all that well enough alone? Complete silence is worse than all that?"

I thought of our critic, Harriet Pease, who wrote for us only once a year, for a summer edition, describing with the purplest of prose the competitions at the county fair. She could spot maturity in a child's finger painting and childishness in an old lady's quilt. She could write paragraphs on the poetic variations of red in a bushel basket of blue-ribbon tomatoes; she could go on for sentences about how impossible it was to describe the simple beauty of Jesus' profile captured in cross-stitch.

"I guess I didn't know you were so unhappy," I said.

Doc stroked my back again. "Oh, I think maybe you did, sweetie," he said. He left my side to sit at the table, and he toyed with the thumb guillotine.

"I'm sorry," I said. "I've had a terrible day." I walked to the bathroom, and to the sink, and closed the door with my foot. I blew my nose with toilet paper. *You'll get over it,* I've told myself over the years when at my most morose. And no sooner have I told myself that than I recognize that I'll be at my most morose again someday. One doesn't become immune from sadness, like after a bout of chicken pox. It's always just ahead, coiled at the periphery of your consciousness. Happy and sad, happy and sad, over and over and over again. How do you bear it?

My hair, unwashed, uncombed, sat atop my head like a neglected wig. As I touched my dragonfly pin, repositioning it, I suddenly, for the first time in years and years, recalled the dragonfly that had lit on my finger when I was eight years old, on a summer afternoon when my Sunday-school teacher had released us children from the church basement into the yard. And with the memory of the feel of the insect's legs on my skin, sticky like flypaper, so much of that day returned to me—the boy who informed me that the bug was called a "snake-eater," frightening me with the prospect of its appetites, paralyzing me with fear despite the bug's frail, needle-slim build.

Part
TEN

· 53 ·

The first obituary I wouldn't write was for Ezekiel Teller. His death had been foretold nearly one hundred years before it occurred. Born weeks too early, he'd been given only weeks to live upon his birth. His parents had rushed a baptism at the hospital, the minister, in a long black robe, standing among weeping nurses in long white skirts as he gently dabbed his dampened fingers against Ezekiel's head, a melon so tiny it'd barely fill a teacup. Ezekiel had survived his difficult birth, and he'd lived his long life without any complication—which is to say, he'd been simple. He'd never married, and he'd never succeeded at any of his many menial jobs. His only visitors in the months before his death had been the old ladies who visited all the churchless shut-ins. He died in the bed he'd likely never shared, at ninety-seven, after a few days down with a nasty cold.

I guess I don't know what I would've written about the unexceptional life of Ezekiel Teller. We'd all known Ezekiel only by his thick head of red hair that never thinned and never grayed. We assumed he'd always dyed it, and that suggestion of vanity intrigued us. That unnatural red hair—spiked and greased to a point, giving the impression of a matchstick struck—had been a kind of institution.

But Doc ceased publication of the County Paragraph only a week after he first told me of his intentions. Ezekiel Teller died on the day of the final issue, the first man of a new many to pass unacknowledged. Certainly other surviving papers were committed to picking up our county's obits, but only in the most perfunctory manner: list of survivors, details of memorial service, photograph published for a nominal fee.

I'd anticipated, at least, weeks of farewell. I'd assumed Doc would announce the paper's approaching end, and we'd only inch toward obscurity, allowing the paper a festive demise. I predicted an enlivening and invigorating debate on the letters page. But the County Paragraph didn't even report its own story. The last issue contained no hint of an ending. It simply did its job one last time. Yes, people were distressed when they heard the paper would no longer publish, but where, in a town without a paper, could such a discussion be recorded? Doc, who for so long had been seen as a weak substitute for his father, unsettled us all with his powerful refusal. As other towns had suffered around us, we had always felt somewhat secure—at least, we'd reasoned, we still had a newspaper while other newspapers in other towns had failed.

At the same time, Daisy punished us too. She quit reading from the red notebook, and each night that our CBs stayed silent, Lenore faded more and more. The cars stopped coming from all around and parking up and down the roads to the Crippled Eighty. The café went back to being closed on Sundays. People stopped mailing Daisy pictures of their missing, stopped sending Lenore gifts of stuffed animals and dolls and ruffled blouses. And just before Christmas, *The Coffins of Little Hope* by Wilton Muscatine was released, and it was as if Lenore's version of his story had never existed.

Though Tiff already had a copy of the book, we nonetheless drove to Omaha to stand in line at midnight, at Mr. Earbrass Booksellers, where the shopkeep was dressed as Madame Digitalis, the hunchbacked palm reader, her head wrapped in a turban. She held forth a silver tray of tiny balsa-wood coffins. You slid the lid forth with your finger, and inside was a licorice zombie. In a corner, a quartet of musicians played gothic instruments—a hurdy-gurdy, a thumb piano, and two kinds of mostly extinct fiddles.

Tiff spent the next several days online following all the hubbub kicked up by the new book: the hot debates between dismissals and praise, the listings of continuity errors ("on page 103 of Book Five, Desiree has a tick-shaped mole on the *left* side of her neck; on page 218 of Book Eleven, it has moved to just beneath her ear! Intentional?"), the copyediting oversights on pages 16, 98, 176, 284, and 512, and much discussion of the gun in the first act that goes off in the third.

And Doc's pride in the artful printing of this complicated book, with its atypical papers and inks and processes, seemed like it might be enough to revive his interest in publishing. I fantasized a grand return of the County Paragraph, with a front-page apology. And everyone, finally, would show the poor boy some respect.

Ezekiel Teller's obit could then run, perhaps even with a full-color photo, his feverish red hair testing the calibrations of the press.

But Doc's interest in the book didn't go much further than his fondling of it. In those first weeks without the newspaper, he confined himself to his house, spending all of every day in his T-shirt and pajama bottoms, letting his beard grow, guzzling coffee directly from the glass pot at the kitchen counter. But this wasn't the decline of a man depressed. He was busy devising a new role for himself, perfecting his sleight of hand, repairing the hinges of faulty trick-boxes, reinforcing the sleeves of his dress shirts for the easy cuffing of playing cards.

Hailey and Sibyl joined us on Christmas Day, and Tiff seemed so grown-up next to Sibyl—Tiff even wore some blue shadow on her eyelids—that I was embarrassed about the childish gift I'd put beneath the tree for her. When I'd bought it at an antique shop just the summer before, I'd been certain she'd love it—a very early piece of Miranda-and-Desiree merchandise. A toy tea set made of thin bisque, decorated with illustrations of the girls having a tea party among rabid and thorny flora and fauna. It sat beneath the tree, taunting in its little-girliness, promising insult.

· 54 ·

I've been a widow for years, yet my catalogs are often addressed to my dead husbands. You wouldn't believe the phone calls I receive, the number of times in a week I have to break the news of my husbands' deaths to salespeople.

One bitterly cold mid-January day, I thumbed through my second husband's brochure for a Namibian safari, investigating the prices for bagging various exotic creatures. The twelve-trophy package was on discount, offering zebras, baboons, jackals, and a "mix and match" of warthogs, ostriches, and bat-eared fox. Neither of my husbands had ever left the country; nor had I. I poured myself some tea, coincidentally, from the raised trunk of a white ceramic elephant, and a postcard slid from the collection of mail in my lap. The picture on the postcard depicted nowhere exotic at all—it was a pancake house, circa 1970, along some highway. The back of it was far more exotic: an invitation from Daisy, asking me to the Crippled Eighty at my earliest convenience.

I went for coffee that morning with my family and said nothing.

"Penny for your thoughts," Ivy said.

"I've always hated that expression," I said. "It's aggressive. And what's worse, it's disguised as a little piece of friendly adorableness in needlepoint stitch."

"Wow, tell us what you *really* think," Ivy said.

"I hate *that* expression even worse," I said. "Practically for the same reasons."

I then caught sight of them all exchanging quick glances and raised eyebrows, as if they were collectively declaring me a senile crank. "You think I don't see that?" I said, making matters worse.

· 55 ·

I ignored Daisy's postcard until the end of January, when the second postcard arrived—this one had a picture of sandpipers on a beach. *Everyone has given up,* Daisy wrote. *It's time to write Lenore's obituary.* In Daisy's mind, the County Paragraph still published, was still preoccupied with every plot twist she orchestrated. On this visit to Daisy, I'd still be what I'd always been.

So that was how I came to sit with her in her kitchen that one afternoon, sipping coffee that tasted burnt, convinced that I could convince her to confess.

But she wanted me to record Lenore's death in order to bring the girl back to life.

"I don't *really* think Lenore is dead," she told me. "I wanted you to write her obituary, and to print it, to wake everybody up. People would be disgusted by it, an obit for Lenore, I know they would. And they'd care about her again. Because, Mrs. Myles, I know that he didn't kill her. He loved her. That's why he took her. She's somewhere alive, and afraid."

"Daisy," I said. "Daisy." I reached across the table so that she could take my hand if she felt so compelled. She did bring her hands to the table, but she kept them folded in front of her. "When you've had a child in your house for any amount of time," I said, "that child is there always. You're still picking up after those children even years after they're not children anymore. You find some piece of petrified gum beneath a dining room chair that you have to chip off with a butter knife. You pick up a kid's drawing from beneath the fridge that fell under there who knows when. A broken toy you always meant to fix, still in a cabinet. Oh," I said, pretending to suddenly remember the barrette in my coat pocket. I'd rehearsed this little lecture and had brought along the pink ruffle that had fixed to a lock of Tiff's thin baby hair with a metal snap. I'd unearthed it only a few days before from a crevice beneath the cushions in the back of the parlor sofa. I explained the discovery to Daisy as I held the ruffle forth in my open palm.

Daisy smiled politely, clearly unmoved. She reached into her own pocket and pulled from it a scrap of paper. She unfolded it and held it before me. It contained one word in the script of a cramped hand: *hypergraphia.*

"Do you know what the word means, Mrs. Myles?" she asked. I said I didn't. "I didn't either," she said, "until I went to the library a few days ago. But I think it's what Lenore had."

"Yes?" I said.

"I would buy her these little diaries from the toy aisle at the grocery store," Daisy said. "I bought every one they had, but then they couldn't get any more, so I bought just regular school notebooks, and she filled them all with what she wrote. And when the notebooks weren't enough, she wrote on anything. The bottom of her shoe. She wrote on a Kleenex once, lightly, so she wouldn't tear it to shreds. She wrote on a gum wrapper, on the side without the foil, in handwriting so small it seemed written with the tip of a needle. And none of it made any sense. It was like poetry."

"The wallpaper," I said, thinking of the plank they'd found in the tree.

"I've always been afraid of someone taking her from me," she said. "If someone had come to the farm and thought she was crazy, they'd say it was my fault. They'd take her away and put her in a school. Her little playhouse, where she wrote on the wallpaper, was already a pile of sticks from the tornado. So I took the notebooks, the diaries, everything she wrote in and wrote on, I took it all into the pasture and burned it, then burned it again. She was furious with me. But I thought I was doing the right thing. I gave her one more notebook, and I said, 'This time,' I said, 'This time write something that makes sense. Write a story,' I said, 'not just words.' And so she wrote what she thought should happen in *The Coffins of Little Hope*. She wrote it in just days. And then she disappeared."

Had Muscatine put this notion in Daisy's head when he'd negotiated for the red notebook? What had been the word he'd used? *Logophilia?* Had he given her a whole vocabulary for inventing Lenore?

"Many imaginative people have had hypergraphia," she said. "I read about it at the library. It's not madness." At first it seemed she looked up and off in thought, but then she touched a fingertip to the corner of her eye, perhaps to release a caught eyelash. As she did so, she went on speaking. "The man who wrote *Alice in Wonderland* had it. And a famous senator. And there was a minister who wrote everything down, everything that happened to him, no matter what, no matter how little it mattered. To him, every minute of his life was worth remembering. He wrote . . . um, I wrote it down somewhere." She opened her hands, and she pushed up her sleeves, looking for the number among the notes she'd written on her skin in ink earlier in the week, a number that had faded to a faint gray. "Thirty-eight," she said, tapping at the number on the heel of her palm. "Thirty-eight million words." Daisy opened her slip of paper again and spelled aloud for me the word *hypergraphia*. I took the cue and opened my notebook, and I wrote the word down.

"There are words for me too," she said. "Or for the me that I'd be if I'd made up Lenore." She took from her other pocket another scrap of paper. "*Factitious disorder with predominantly psychological signs and symptoms*. Or possibly *delusional disorder—a persecutory type*. Or there's *phantasy,* spelled with a *ph* instead of an *f*."

I wrote it all down.

"I'm aware of the charges that could be filed against me and the fines I could be made to pay." She took from her cardigan pocket yet another slip of paper. "*Conspiracy,*" she read. "*Making a false report to authorities*. Any number of misdemeanors and felonies. Thousands and thousands of dollars you could make me pay. And you could put me in jail. There are people who are demanding it. People who don't even know me."

"They think *you* wrote in the red notebook," I said.

Without speaking, Daisy slowly, listlessly collected all the slips of paper before her, one by one, folding them, returning each to her pockets.

"Did you know my father, Mrs. Myles?" she asked. "At all? When you wrote his obituary?"

"No," I said. When writing the obit of Daisy's father thirteen years before, I'd naturally begun with the farm. We'd all driven by it, noticed its peculiar name burned into the sign at the end of the driveway. We'd known its crooked vein of broken fences. Those of us who took walks along country roads had plundered the unpicked mulberries from a tree in a ditch along the Crippled Eighty's pastureland. We'd remarked upon the strange ornamentation of the vegetable garden—a rusting claw-footed bathtub among the tomato plants; a marble obelisk, most likely thieved from one of the old farmers' cemeteries, among the stalks of sweet corn. A scarecrow, his face an old patchwork quilt, wore a denim leisure suit and loomed above an old elevator gate propped on its side, up which pea plants vined.

I remember visiting Daisy in the days after her father died, his heart having given out. He'd died in an act that could've been defiance. The neighboring farmer had irrigated with a central pivot—a segmented steel centipede-like sprinkler that stretched across the acres and inched along on motorized wheels. The pivot's nozzle had stuck and had blasted water in a steady stream onto the Crippled Eighty. Nothing but weeds and prairie grasses had come to grow on that section of the farm, but Daisy's father had nonetheless gotten up on the fence and lifted a shovel above his head in order to slam it against the nozzle, to redirect its aim back onto the neighbor's cornfield.

Back then I had sat at this kitchen table with my notebook, long before I'd known anything at all about Daisy. She had told me how he would take a hose to gopher holes to fill them with water to drown the pesky creatures that chewed on the leaves of his lettuce in the garden. She had told me that when the windmill stopped pumping up water, he'd shoot his rifle into the deep hole in the ground to break up whatever had clogged the aquifer. He would concoct his own poisons and record in a notebook their effect on the weeds that crept into his garden, and he collected bugs, different varieties, that he'd toss into a shoebox to watch them battle. She had told me many other things too, but the details of his quiet violence against the earth were what I had put in my obit.

"I wrote you a letter after the obituary ran," Daisy said. "But I never sent it." And from her pocket she took yet one more piece of paper. I opened it and read its few lines: *Ms. Obituary Writer, I hope you never have to know such illness, and I hope your own obituary does not attempt to define your entire life with a portrait of your senility.*

"I never meant any disrespect," I said. "I never do. Quite the opposite. I don't believe it's at all a kindness to make good-intentioned revisions."

This was not the first time I'd been confronted for an obituary, and not the first time I'd given my spiel about *good-intentioned revisions*. But it was the first time that my defense had sounded to me, to even my good ear, quite weak. I went on, "I think people should be remembered for the ways they lived their lives. They should be remembered for who they were."

"He wasn't, though," she said. She seemed not at all angry. She sniffled from the cold air in the room. "He wasn't who he was anymore, I mean. After my mother left us, he wasn't the man who'd taken care of me. Something was always happening to change him. But how could you have known that? You never knew him. Ever."

She was lonely, was all. I could see that now. That loneliness, the emptiness of her house, had been the reason why Daisy had not at first bothered to hang a girl's clothes in the closet or to put up posters on the bedroom wall. Daisy had invented Lenore from the echoes that bounced from all the bare corners. To see the little girl where no little girl had ever been, she had to invent a child who'd possessed nothing. She had to invent a girl who had had only the clothes on her back.

I admit to a fantasy of my own. I thought if I could coax Daisy to reveal everything, it would demand we revive the newspaper. Doc would have to print a special edition, and if he printed a special edition, he'd then print another and another. The whole thing would rustle Doc from his too-early retirement.

"I think you've always wanted to get caught, Daisy," I said. "You didn't even try. You put it all together as you went along. You've just wanted someone to talk you into telling the truth. Tell *me* the truth. We'll take care of you." I reached across and took Daisy's hand, clutching it hard. "That's what we do. We take care of each other. Tell me the truth."

I'm not even now sure who I meant when I said *we*. Did I mean my family? My town?

But there could be no truth that would serve us. If it had turned out that Lenore had, against all logic, existed, and that her suffering had been real, and that so had Daisy's, and that none of us had done enough after all, we would've abandoned that notion too. It would've been too overwhelming, too tragic.

Daisy took her hand back. "After I burned her notebooks last summer," Daisy continued, looking down at the table, running her finger through spilled sugar, "Lenore would hide to do her writing. In trees, in closets. One afternoon I looked all over for her. I was as scared as I've ever been. Hours I looked for her, it seemed like. I looked outside, inside. I cried, calling her name, looking at the walls. I begged her to come out. *Come out, come out, wherever you are*. It got dark.

Then all of a sudden, she started yelling for me. I yelled back. She yelled, 'I'm in the basement.' She was hysterical. She was hiding under an old bed. Her hair was caught. She'd caught her hair in the springs, and she couldn't get it uncaught. Neither could I. I had to cut her loose with scissors."

I wrote down *springs, hair, scissors*. "Then it would still be there, wouldn't it?" I said.

"What?" she said.

"If Lenore's hair caught in a bedspring this summer," I said, "then it would still be in the bedspring." Anyone who has ever been a mother is used to catching liars in lies—children of all ages often underestimate their mothers' powers of deduction. It nonetheless made me uncomfortable, this kind of confrontation, as if *I* were the one telling the fib.

"Yes," Daisy said after a moment. She held my glance. Had I caught her, or had she caught me? Was I being led to the basement, and beneath a bed, to find a telltale lock of white-blond hair that I could carry back to the villagers?

But she led me nowhere. As she looked back down to her hands, I could see her letting loose the thread of our conversation, drifting away from the practical, burdensome weight of bedsprings and wisps of hair. I clipped my earring back on, returned my watch to my wrist. I pushed the dragonfly pin back into the braid atop my head.

"Lenore's hair is probably getting so long," Daisy said.

Rapunzel, Rapunzel, I thought, picturing Lenore peacefully trapped in a tower.

· 56 ·

We left Daisy alone the rest of the winter. Spring came late.

Doc's beard still grew, untrimmed, his hair long and uncombed. He'd sold the printing factory in the country for far less than it was worth, and he had begun work on converting the newspaper offices into his little shop of oddities. He'd been inspired by a store in Kansas City that sold drawers full of porcelain doorknobs and tin coffee cans full of drawer pulls and a few faulty-wired vintage lamps that didn't light but could hold candlesticks beneath their stained-glass shades. He planned to call the shop the County Paragraph and sell off the newspaper's history as art—its brass and wood-block letters and numbers from printing presses; old pages of advertisements and comic strips suitable for framing.

He took me for a tour of these offices I'd known all my life. I leaned on my umbrella and stepped forward, puzzling over the architecture. The owner of the hardware store on the other side of the town square had been helping nights to build new walls and knock out old ones.

Doc's enthusiasm for the project had rendered him incapable of feeling any guilt of any kind. He'd given his former employees severance pay; he'd arranged for some of our writers to freelance with other newspapers. He'd attended to his conscience all he'd felt he'd needed to.

"I want to show you these," he said, but as he fussed with a box, my attention was drawn to the trash can. Atop the overflow sat a very unexceptional shaving brush resting in a useless, broken mug. The brush had a tortoiseshell handle, and its bristles were of boar's hair. I knew because it had been my father's, and I had bought it for him. I'd given it as a birthday gift one year so that he could shave at the office when the news kept him from coming home at night or took him from the house before dawn. The gift had had manipulative intent; I'd meant to cause a pang of regret. I'd meant for him to toss the mug and brush away upon first sight, to take me in his arms, and to apologize for always putting the paper first, always rushing off to follow runaways, houses afire, public drunkenness, devastating storms rapidly approaching. Instead, he'd thought me practical.

"Glass-plate negatives," Doc said, taking one from the box and holding it up to a stream of light from the front window. "This one's of an old baseball team. Look at their socks."

"Yes, look at their socks," I said, looking down

at my shoes. All the revisions to these walls and floors I'd known for decades made me nervous and claustrophobic. One good blast from a sparkler bomb and the whole shoddy operation would shatter into twigs.

I shrugged. "Well, I'm off," I said. "I have a cake turning to poison in the pickup." From the bakery down the street I'd bought strawberry angel food with a seven-minute frosting, its peaks whipped from real egg whites, tempting salmonella.

The late-winter months had been so harsh—blizzard after blizzard, the same dirty drifts thick in our yards and streets for weeks—that these early hints of summer had brought everyone out, especially the children. They fled from their houses and schoolrooms with a vengeance, racing their bikes down the middle of streets and covering every inch of pavement with chalk drawings. On the sidewalk in front of the newspaper offices, I opened my umbrella, though there'd only been clouds, no rain. As I walked away, I stepped through the squares of a hopscotch grid.

"You're not going to be able to stay mad at me about all this," Doc said from where he leaned in the doorway.

"I'm already not mad at you," I said. Standing within the end square, I pivoted on the ball of my right foot to turn to him. "But I don't much care for the direction that beard's going, to be honest."

"Just so happens, I'm cutting it off." He nonetheless stroked his beard possessively. "I told Hailey I'd shave before the wedding." I cocked my head and raised an eyebrow, as if to say, *Wedding?* He smiled. "The plan was to tell everybody tonight at dinner. I bought a fifty-dollar bottle of champagne, so you can all congratulate us."

Again I cocked my head, as if to say, *Fifty dollars?* He had to have gone out of town for it—there wasn't a fifty-dollar bottle of champagne to be bought within miles. "How long ago did you propose, anyway?" I said.

"I asked her a few weeks ago. But she only just said 'yes' yesterday. Finally."

"She was smart to take her time," I said. "You should never rush into a second marriage."

"Essie, we were *kids* together, for God's sake," he said. "We've known each other for thirty years."

How could that possibly be true? I thought.

"When we tell you tonight," Doc said, "act surprised."

"Oh, it's no act," I said. "I'm constantly surprised." I proceeded to my pickup, and once inside, I opened the cake box to tear at the angel food and eat pieces of it with my fingertips.

It was only May, but I heard the electric snapping of a chain of firecrackers from somewhere nearby, and I was pleased the children were speeding toward the holiday, all their fingers and thumbs still intact. I decided to take a drive along the country roads I'd avoided most of the winter. I would visit the Crippled Eighty and share my cake with Daisy. The last time I'd seen her, way back on that cold January afternoon, I'd promised to look after her. And yet I hadn't. None of us had.

· 57 ·

Even before no one answered my rapid knocking at Daisy's door, I suspected no reply. The house had always had the aspects of a ruin—right down to its cement gargoyle broken in the weedy, overgrown rose garden near the front porch—but it seemed somehow that my huffing and puffing would blow the whole house down.

I've never been visited by my many ghosts, much to my regret. In my solid, incredulous presence, phantoms flee séances. The planchettes of Ouija boards go deadly still. But in old age, you can nearly convince yourself you're not alone. You hear, in your bad ear, voices among the sounds of your own blood pumping through your veins. Without your glasses, in the mushing of shapes, you see shadows and movements of figures not there.

I knocked again, and it seemed the knocking

roused something inside the house. I pressed my ear against the glass of the door but could only hear the minor tintinnabulation that had lately become frequent. Sometimes my damaged hearing produced a buzz, a steady creak, like a cricket in a wall. I'd become affectionate toward it.

I leaned over the porch railing to see into the window. I saw a rag doll all ripped up, facedown on the floor, its stuffing everywhere but inside of it.

I opened the front door slowly. "Daisy, the door was unlocked," I called out, stepping inside, setting the cake box on an end table. "You should lock up, darling, even in the country." I crept right past the kitchen without once glancing inside; had I looked, I would've seen enough to warn me away—the low cupboard doors wide open, the floor covered in emptied packages and boxes. I would've seen the paw prints frantic in the flour that had spilled from a gnawed-upon sack.

Up from the basement came a low, slow howl that didn't sound canine at all. I pictured Daisy on her back beneath a bed, every strand of her hair caught in the springs as she starved to death in a mad metaphorical gesture. "Daisy," I said. "Answer me." I descended each steep step carefully, one hand on the wall, the other on my umbrella for support. I could feel the umbrella's tube warping from my scrawny weight. As I reached the bottom of the stairs, even before my eyes adjusted to the dim light let in by the window above the washing machine, I met the stare of a pair of eyes that in my memory burn deep red. And then I saw another pair. Then another. I saw the dogs among the torn boxes and shattered mason jars of Daisy's canned vegetables—the howling came from a dog curled up in pain along the wall. I would learn later that that he, among a few of the other hounds, had devoured shards of glass among the pickled watermelon and beets.

The dogs stayed still, then stepped forward into a shaft of murky daylight, their hackles up on the backs of their necks like porcupine quills. They growled with clenched jaws, keeping their voices rumbling with threat in their throats. I stepped backward up the stairs.

"I'll leave you alone, gentlemen," I said in my best approximation of a harmless, high-pitched, girlish lilt. Because what's the most frightening thing about being frightened by dogs? Fear itself, of course, and their famous, brutal sense of it. In trying to hold my shaking breath, to disguise it from the dogs, my heart beat faster and my breathing shook more. *Be calm, damn it,* I advised myself. "I'm all gristle," I sang. "Not worth the trouble." The dogs at first matched my wary movement, only inching forward, their heads and necks lowered. Their instincts were off—they were suspicious of my fear. But before I reached the top of the stairs, it was *me* matching *their* rhythms and speed—they began to bark with barks hoarse and strangled, and they tumbled over each other's many legs as they fought in hopes of being the first to snap my brittle-boned ankles between their teeth.

I reached the door soon enough to slam it behind me. As I leaned back, I felt the hard smack of dogs throwing themselves against the door. I heard the weaker of them falling, rolling back down the stairs, only to race back up them again. Their claws on the door seemed to follow my spine. Their barking, which had grown maniacal, drowned out the sounds of more dogs coming down from the upstairs. I caught sight of this new pack soon enough to run, looking for any entryway with a door, of which I discovered there were many. There were doors to hallways, and in the middle of hallways, more doors than were at all necessary when one wasn't being attacked by rabid mutts.

The dogs knew the house better than I did, and with every slammed door they would quickly reroute. I finally reached the kitchen, leaving my own prints in the flour. As I ran out the back door, throwing it shut behind me, my sleeve caught in the handle of the screen, just as my sleeves have hooked on handles and doorknobs hundreds of times before, in that little gap in the material beneath the button of the cuff. It was only a swift snag, followed by an easy release, but enough to tumble me down the few cement steps to the sidewalk, a very short fall that somehow managed to break both my ankles.

The silence of the dogs disturbed me, seemed strategic, so I ignored the great pain in my step and limped forth at a frantic clip, cringing and leaning on my umbrella, practically skipping forward to keep as much of myself off my feet as possible, weighing the option of simply collapsing in the grass to be attacked. When I heard the echo of the dogs barking in the open air and saw a flock of swallows rustled from a bush near the house, I ran to my pickup, wailing in agony. The dogs reached me just as I opened the passenger-side door, and teeth tore at my long skirt, then sank into my leg. As I crawled inside, I managed to fight them off with my umbrella, sticking the end of it into a one-eyed dog's one good eye and beating it against the head of another one. I pulled the door forward, clocking the head of a particularly wolfish-looking beast. He yelped and pulled away, and I managed to get the door closed. They continued to bark, throwing their bodies against the truck so hard it rocked on its chassis.

My doctor would later tell me that the fall had probably produced only thin fractures; it was my mad dash on the fractures that had cracked the bones good. But that afternoon, as I lay back, stretched out on the pickup's seat, convinced I was trapped, the pain of my ankles seemed to pulse through all my extremities. I had no sense of what was broken and what wasn't. Throughout my old age, I'd feared an undignified end—from time to time, I'd considered moments in my recent past that would've made for an appropriate demise. But this end, this final one, if that was what it was, couldn't have been more fitting if I'd orchestrated it. Attacked by feral dogs, hobbled on the Crippled Eighty.

I managed to pull myself up by the steering wheel to look out across the yard. The dogs had stopped attacking the truck, distracted by the smells of the outdoors, wandering in a manic path toward the field or the barn. They seemed worse off than just wild and abandoned. They were covered in scars, their coats spotted with bald patches. One dog's tail dragged behind him as if busted. Another dog was bereft of both ears.

From my purse on the floor of the pickup I took my pill box, and from it four aspirin. I swallowed them without water. I looked at myself in my rearview mirror; it was a good thing, I decided, that this hadn't done me in after all. I wouldn't want them finding me so unpresentable, my lipstick smeared across my mouth like a drunken harlot's. I felt around in the turmoil of my hair, my fingertips seeking my dragonfly pin. I'd lost it too.

I tried to calculate how many years I'd worn that pin in my hair. No one had given the pin to me. In my middle age, I'd gone to an obit writers' conference in St. Louis, held in a respectable hotel. Though the conference had ended, I'd stayed on. I'd been long widowed, and my son had married, and I'd sat alone in the lobby one morning having a breakfast of one soft-boiled egg and a tall wineglass filled to the brim with a Bloody Mary. I'd worn an evening-time cocktail dress, black, with black pumps, my hair freshly teased from an early-morning appointment in the hotel's salon. I'd wanted to be one of those melancholy, strange, and lovely women you see in hotels and wonder about. But I hadn't sensed anyone wondering about me, not even the only other woman alone in the lobby, the woman in the leopard-print stole reading a paperback romance and inelegantly eating slices of an apple from a baggie she'd taken from her purse. Where was everyone off to? I'd wondered. Who were they meeting? I had ordered another Bloody Mary, then another, but I hadn't gotten at all tipsy, though the waiter raised an eyebrow at me when I accidentally knocked over the egg it was taking me forever to eat. After breakfast, in the hotel's gift shop off the lobby, I'd considered the matronly dragonfly pin that rested on a blue-velvet pillow, its wings weighted by its tacky cluster of glass sapphires. I'd had a premonition right then, seeing it heavy on my head in my old age, snared flightless in the silver coils of my hair.

My still-young self invented me right then and there—the formidable hag I'd make someday. I'd pictured myself quirky in men's trousers, stewed on home-bottled cucumber wine. Maybe I'd smoke those womanly cigars as, my pants cuffed, my feet bare, I wrote an autobiographical novel that exposed all those responsible for my heartbreak. They'd find me dead on my sofa, having finally gotten around to reading *Anna Karenina*. "She died with that dragonfly pin right where it always was, in her hair above her left ear, the ear she heard the best through," my obit writer would say.

But back then, I hadn't imagined myself living so very long—it had seemed to tempt fate to envision myself in my eighties. I just didn't see myself as having that kind of luck. So I hadn't bought the dragonfly pin, and not buying it had nagged at me for years. Sometime later I'd called the hotel to see if they'd still had that pin. Not only had they no longer had it, but the gift shop had long since been turned into a cocktail lounge. So when I'd come upon a reasonable facsimile in an antique shop in Iowa, I'd bought it, probably a good twenty years after those Bloody Marys in the hotel lobby.

My dogs noticed I'd survived, and they returned, bringing on a new attack. It turns out they weren't bored with me after all, those darling pooches. As the truck shimmied from the effects of their resumed fury, I took a tissue to my lips and reapplied my lipstick, dotting my lips with a shade of cinnamon-plum that had been discontinued two years before but that the pharmacist had helped me to stock up on. I scooted behind the steering wheel and started the pickup, wincing from the throbbing not just from my broken ankles but also from the rather noteworthy chomp a lupine-looking bitch had blessed my right leg with. Maybe I'd wake up as a werewolf, freshly immortal but feeble from rabies.

It hurt too much to press either of my feet down on the gas pedal, so I put the tip of my umbrella to it and drove myself through the open gate of the Crippled Eighty, and to the hospital, the dogs chasing alongside much of the way.

Part

After being released from the hospital a few days after my mauling, and into my sister's nursing home for a week, I loved to tell people I was having a stint in rehab. And that was indeed what the doctors called it, *rehabilitation,* my ankles in braces, a nurse, his handsome face marred by an outdated mustache, attending to my recovery. I was far too weak to not fall in love with the muscular Carlos, who wore a tiny gold key on a chain around his neck.

"It's silly, I suppose," he said when I asked him about it as he wheeled me down to the next unit to visit my sis, "but it means a lot to my little girl." We calculated together: about the same hour I'd been attacked at the Crippled Eighty, he'd been putting on his Sunday best in order to attend a "purity dance" with his seventeen-year-old daughter. With his wife, he'd brushed up on his waltzing in front of their bedroom mirror, then he'd taken Maria, in her prom-night formal, to a hotel ballroom in Omaha. They'd had a dinner of broiled chicken, then a ceremony during which Maria, with a white rose, had vowed chastity until her wedding day. "The day I give her to her husband at the altar," he said, his voice catching, "I will lose this key. I will give it to the new man in her life."

Normally I'd scoff, cynical of such virginal pageantry, but for that week, Carlos, and all the others looking after me at the Manor, were the people most dear to me in my life. They knew what was best for me, better than I knew myself, and I was frequently intoxicated with affection for these strangers. I'd sit in my chair by the window, feeling warmly even toward the gardener so committed to keeping the courtyard blooming.

Tiff lent me her iPod after loading it with Erik Satie and Camille Saint-Saens, which she'd discovered after searching for "soothing classical music," and I would listen as I sat with my sister in the afternoons, shutting out the noise of her soap operas, the iPod's plugs nestled in my ears.

"I keep thinking I should thin out my things," I told Lydia.

"You have old love letters," Lydia said, taking a piece of jellied candy from the box in her lap and biting into it with sudden agitation.

"No," I said, thinking instead of all the years of little snippets of notes still on notepads in drawers, reminding me to do things I never bothered doing. Recipes, in a tin box, for dishes I never cooked. Expired pills in the apothecary. Shoelaces still in the package. Books on the writing of books, for the novel I never began. My family will spend days lifting items from the dust, considering their worth, tossing them away. Lifting, considering, tossing. Toward the end of their task, they'll sigh at so many of my things, rolling their eyes, wondering how I'd not recognized that I'd never needed to keep any of it.

When first provided with the wheelchair, when I'd been uncertain that I'd live long enough to fully bounce back, I felt sentenced to a horror show. It seemed I'd not made it through life on both feet, and at eighty-three years old, such a discovery can be existentially disappointing. But as soon as I felt a recovery creeping up, I found that the wheelchair offered a security I was too frightened to leave behind. I began to enjoy the sympathy I had at first rejected. When you don't really need it, a wheelchair can feel quite powerful.

As the end of my rehabilitation neared, Doc visited to tease me with a trick involving three upended coffee cups. Doc's ruined career seemed to suit him. His shop still far from completion, the delay, at least, had put off the possibility of the shop's failure. In the meantime, he tended bar at a tavern called Buzzard's, cultivating among the townsfolk the appearance of having fallen on hard luck, a reputation he appeared to find glamorous.

"That one," I said, tapping at the bottom of one of the cups, nothing beneath it, and nothing was beneath my second pick either. And then, there, under the last cup, I discovered my dragonfly pin, the bug swatted, mangled, its wings askew, its head off-kilter.

"The dogs must've batted it around a little," Doc told me. "It wasn't too far from the kitchen door. Probably flew right out of your head when you fell."

My pack of dogs, Doc had learned, had escaped from a farm a few miles up the road from the Crippled Eighty, where men and women from all over had gathered for basement dogfights. The dogs had been kept in cages meant for chickens until a lover's spat between the farmer and a lady truck driver had led to her running through the basement, unlatching cage doors.

When Daisy had left the Crippled Eighty, left it for good, whatever day that had been, she'd opened her own doors and windows, either to let an ill wind in or to let it out, and the dogs, like story-time wolves, had eventually invited themselves in in her absence.

"I'll take it to the jeweler to be fixed," Doc offered, but I refused, charmed by the wreckage of the pin. It too had survived our attack. I returned the cockeyed thing to its place in my hair.

· 59 ·

Ivy and Tiff kindly offered to take me in, but I chose instead to return to my house and allow others to be bothered with my well-being. I signed up for any and every social service I was entitled to, and I spent my days accepting and dismissing visitors—a mobile librarian brought me my books, churchy volunteers stopped by with covered dishes, nurses put my pills in little paper cups, and an eldercare counselor analyzed my temperament.

And Tiff steered me toward health with her experiments in the kitchen. I'd told her about Lydia's cookbook, a sacred text, practically, leatherbound like a book of potions, its bindings and stitches strained with all the notes and addendums Lydia had stuffed into it over the years, its brittle corners singed, its edges splattered from being too near the stove. The margins of the pages demonstrated a Lenorian level of hypergraphia, Lydia having kept detailed notes and corrections, not because she'd worried she'd forget (I'd never once witnessed her glancing at a recipe) but because she'd thought it might be appreciated by her daughter. Her daughter, however, had married poorly, ruined her life early on, and thickened herself on bad food from drive-through windows. She unhesitatingly relinquished the book to Tiff when Tiff visited her to ask to borrow it.

"You should keep it, darling," Lydia's daughter told Tiff as she pulled the book from the back of a cupboard she had to stand on a footstool to reach, the footstool's joints fairly screeching from the weight. She looked at Tiff askance with a quick, dismissive summing-up. "You need to get a little meat on your bones."

By the end of that summer, I'd abandoned the wheelchair for the most part, a cane now in each hand, and Tiff had taken over my kitchen. She improvised on some of Lydia's recipes when they called for ingredients no longer easily accessible at our beleaguered local grocery—kohlrabi, gooseberries, lard.

"What's it need more of ?" Tiff said one August afternoon, chewing a bite of peach pie with concern. We sat at the kitchen table with just two spoons, digging in without bothering to slice or serve it.

"Well, it needs a little *less of*," I said. "It's too tart, isn't it?" I wasn't being critical, and Tiff knew that. She knew I only wanted the best for her—for her to take Lydia's recipes and become, someday, not a good wife (or not only a good wife) but a five-star restaurateur in a city of importance.

"Ugh," she said, leaving her spoon in the pie. She threw herself back in the kitchen chair and shoved her hands in her pockets. "Because I rushed the peaches. They weren't quite ripe."

"You picked them?"

Tiff bit her lip and admitted, "The Crippled Eighty. We trespassed." Tiff then furthered her confession: she'd lied to Ivy the day before, claiming to be going to the river to swim with some girlfriends, in a van driven by one of the girls' older sister. But there'd been no van, no girls, no river. A boy named Trevor, who'd just turned sixteen, just gotten his license, and just bought a 1983 Mustang off his brother, had driven her to the Eighty, the two of them alone. Torrential downpours of recent days had pushed rivers and creeks past their banks, and a drainage ditch that wound through a valley of the Crippled Eighty overflowed, turning the pasture into a small lake, noisy and musical with the croaking of frogs.

Trevor went in first, but only up to his knees, instantly sinking, his feet clogged in the mud. He stepped back out, scratching his legs.

"I pictured a nice dip in some fresh rainwater," he said. "I'm not letting you go in. It's probably full of pesticides, rolling down from the fields." He looked off at the neighboring farms, his hand over his eyes to block the sun, and Tiff hoped he kept looking off and away so he wouldn't catch her staring. Trevor was scrawny and not at all sporty, but he had a deep voice, deeper even than Doc's, and he seemed a little embarrassed by it. He spoke mostly in a hush when he felt the need to speak at all, which wasn't often.

They sat in the sun on a quilt in the weeds, and Trevor ran his finger over her outstretched leg, spelling out *Trev and Tiff.* He then spelled, on her other leg, *at the beach.* Tiff had turned fourteen a few months before, and it had begun to nag at her that she'd never been kissed. She'd yet to hold hands with a boy. Other girls were already being pressured to do things they didn't want to do, and though she certainly didn't want that, she did wish a boy liked her enough to at least make things a little difficult.

"I have kind of a date this weekend," he said. "I'm just telling you so you don't think it's a secret." He lay on his back, closed his eyes, and linked his fingers over his naked chest. "I'll take *you* on a date someday, when you're older and your mom lets you out without having to sneak." Tiff's first instinct was to make a joke of it, to be funny, but she thought better of it and kept mum. Her silence seemed to rouse Trevor. He sat back up on his elbow and traced the name of his date on her leg. Tiff shrugged her shoulders, unable to decipher it, and he traced the name again. Finally he said, "Mazda. Mazda Capshaw. She plays the oboe."

Trevor, first-chair alto sax, had been Tiff's mentor—the spring before ninth grade, if you were interested in joining the high school band, you were assigned an older student to initiate you into the militaristic regimens of marching and pep. Tiff had dropped out within a few days but had continued to swap texts with Trevor.

As the boy napped on the quilt, Tiff plucked a dandelion and rubbed its yellow onto the inside of her wrist. She lay back to look at the house on the hill, and when she squinted, blurring her vision, she could set the gray place ablaze with the afternoon sunlight. Tiff drifted off. She woke only minutes later as the sun slipped behind a cloud, Daisy's ghost working out from her short dream and suddenly there, standing over them, or slipping through them, in the feathering of shade that touched her skin. When the sun's heat returned, savage against her, her sweat stinging her eyes, she summoned Daisy's ghost, longing for the soft, swift relief of the cloud. Tiff didn't mind; she wasn't frightened.

· *60* ·

Had Daisy only been haunting the house all along? Maybe years from now, people will doubt that any of it happened, will believe that we invented not just Lenore but Daisy too. How could anyone have been so gullible? they'll ask. Tiff, as an old woman herself, my dragonfly pin poked into her white coils of hair, could show them the scrap of wallpaper she'd saved, the handwriting following the pattern of roses. Everyone would just accuse us all of forgery.

The week of Doc and Hailey's wedding in early September, Tiff and Trevor decided to return to the Eighty to steal more peaches, sweeter ones, and they invited me along. Tiff had still not told Ivy about the boy, but not because she courted danger. "If Ivy knew Trevor drove me around, she'd get fussy just because she thinks she's supposed to," Tiff explained as Trevor drove too quickly down the loose-gravel road, his engine rattling with disrepair. "I'll tell her it's nothing, which is the truth, but she'll make it into something."

I was happy to get to be the one to not disapprove. In her looking after me when my ankles were broken, Tiff had demonstrated a curt and graceful impatience that had hastened my progress and put her in my trust. She had not let me be lazy or petulant.

But no romance had seemed to progress between Tiff and Trevor over the summer. His one date with Mazda Capshaw had become other dates with Mazda Capshaw, and he'd turned big-brotherly toward Tiff, often teasing her without any hints of flirtation. After every word Trevor uttered that afternoon, Tiff rolled her eyes either from annoyance or from the unwieldy blink of her false eyelashes. She was practicing getting used to the lashes and their glue, their fluttering getting all tangled up, dragging down her lids. She was to be the lone bridesmaid at Doc and Hailey's wedding and she now wore empty Pepsi cans as curlers—all week she'd experimented with styles featured in a bridal magazine, seeking the classiest wedding-day hairdo.

Ivy had taken it upon herself to make her brother's wedding unique. She'd used her connections at the Myrtle Kingsley Fitch

Foundation to allow us the use of the little church in Lemontree where Myrtle had been baptized, and in which she'd been raised. Though Myrtle had never herself married, she'd set her limpid but famed novel there, *A Prairie Wedding Among the Radishes*, describing the church's windows painted to look like stained glass, its beams bent to resemble flying buttresses. The church's piano was a remnant of a defunct saloon, two stray bullets from a gunfight still embedded in its wood. Doc and Hailey's wedding would technically be in violation of the law, as the weathered chapel flaked with lead paint and had been closed to the public for years. To remedy its condition would require the church be covered with an enormous tent to contain the removal of the whitewash that was chipping away, all on its own, into the air.

The front gate to the Crippled Eighty was chained shut, but its brittle, rusty hinges were easily unpinned, so Trevor had it open in less than a minute. He drove us onto the land and toward the small orchard of peach trees. I looked at the house as we passed, the place forever, in my imagination, beset with dogs ready to spring from around any corner. The hollyhocks were in bloom beneath the front window—my sister and I, as girls, had picked hollyhocks from our own flower garden, a garden my mother had once cultivated, and we'd braided them into dolls we cradled in our arms.

A cloud of humidity near the orchard was indistinguishable from the swarms of gnats. We stepped from Trevor's car, and to the trees, and we collected the peaches in pillowcases. Earlier in the summer, Tiff had come to the farm to tie blue and pink and yellow ribbons to the branches. Tiny fragments of broken mirror were attached to the ribbons, and when they spun in the wind, sunlight sparked against the glass, to frighten off the squirrels that would otherwise eat the peaches right on the tree, right off the stems, down to the stones. Many of the nearly white peaches had already fallen to the ground, the humid, sugary scent drawing flies, beautiful ones, fat flies with iridescent golden backs like scarabs.

· *61* ·

When Hailey, a few days before her wedding, invited me to visit her store to select a dress, I made the mistake of mentioning a dress that had been hanging unworn in my closet ever since my second husband's death. I'd bought the dress for our ten-year anniversary. For a party for my husband and me on a Saturday, Doc had reserved the garden and gazebo of the bed-and-breakfast and had ordered a tiered cake to be dotted with candied violets. For the occasion, I'd bought the least somber dress in Mrs. Oliver's—an apricot-colored number of linen and organza.

And a few days before the party, my husband suffered a heart attack, was hospitalized in Omaha, seemed he might be on the mend, but died three weeks later.

Hailey, sitting next to me on the sofa, put her hand on my hand. *"That* dress," she said. "That's the dress you should wear." She poked me with a pin unwittingly; she had some stuck in her cuff from a day of alterations.

"No," I said. "I think it would be bad luck."

"Not at all," she said, squeezing my hand harder, the pin gouging me more.

"Ouch," I said. "Pins and needles, sweetheart, pins and needles."

"Oh, dear," Hailey said. She plucked the pin from her cuff and stabbed it into a piece of saltwater taffy in the candy dish on the coffee table.

I found myself wondering what would be most memorable about Tiff's own wedding someday, and I pictured it as people tend to picture the sublime futures of their children. I imagined her not in a chapel in decline, with its toxic dust motes stirring in the beams of sunlight, but in a public garden, perhaps, with white swans and black swans in a small lake and trees in April bloom. Her gown would have lace and a train and a veil.

After my chat with Hailey, I went home and unzipped my anniversary dress from its vinyl wrapper. I put it on and modeled it for myself in the mirror. As I gazed upon this dress, which wasn't at all the type of dress I'd ever wear, I grew fond of its delicate formality, its lady-like insistence. My slightest movement sent it into conniptions, and I admired the flounce and wiggle of the organza. The dress had a life all its own.

You were young, I thought, not *once* but *always* before, always always, every day before the day just passed. You were young only minutes ago.

My thanks to Alice Tasman and Greg Michalson, for their generosity and friendship, and their attention to this novel. Thanks also to Fred Ramey, Caitlin Hamilton Summie, and all at Unbridled Books and the Jean Naggar Agency for their support. Thanks to Gerald Shapiro and Judy Slater, for our many bookish conversations over the years; to Dr. David Hansen of the University of Nebraska-Lincoln for consulting with me on the psychological condition of my fictional characters; and to Claire Kirch, whose intrepid journalism offered insights into the particulars of small-town presses covertly printing famous novels.

Thanks to Rodney Rahl, an endless source of practical information, wit, and off-kilter intelligence, upon which I greatly rely. It's difficult and troubling to imagine what direction my novels would take without him.

Thanks to Janet Lura and Leslie Prisbell, who are constantly fielding my emails asking for advice on technical matters and issues of character development; and to Joy Ritchie, Hilda Raz, Prairie Schooner, and the University of Nebraska-Lincoln English Department. Thanks also to Kate Bernheimer, Maud Casey, Lauren Cerand, Emily

Danforth, Chuck and Mary Mignon, Justin Wolta, and the Chittendens of Emile Street, for their various and sundry acts of encouragement and assistance in the writing of this novel. And endless thanks to my parents, Larry and Donita Schaffert.

Center Point Publishing

600 Brooks Road ● PO Box 1
Thorndike ME 04986-0001 USA

(207) 568-3717

US & Canada:
1 800 929-9108
www.centerpointlargeprint.com